Freedom Flight

By Alan Van Ormer

Prologue

Rye Tyler's life changed on July 12, 1862 in the Murfreesboro prison. He remembered every detail of his capture on that day and his freedom the next. Deep down, Rye knew he shouldn't set foot in the town, but he needed one more piece of information. He hoped to gather it soon and deliver it to Nathan Bedford Forrest.

But, best laid plans sometimes don't work. Union Soldiers had captured him.

Rye slowly dropped his revolver to the ground and lifted his arms. A Union soldier stepped over and snapped Rye's left arm behind his back. The other three soldiers laughed at the pop in his left shoulder. Pain surged through his arm, and it hung limp.

"Chain him," a Union sergeant blustered.

Another soldier lugged heavy chains and wrapped them around Rye's wrists, then bent down and tied his ankles. The pain in Rye's left shoulder required him to hold the chains taut with his right arm. The soldier pushed him ahead, forcing him on a frenzied pace.

Murfreesboro, Tennessee, thirty-five miles southeast of Nashville, was the destination. Two days ago Rye provided Nathan Bedford Forrest information about the town, an important depot on the Nashville and Chattanooga Railroad. The colonel had asked him to gather more intelligence that would assist in an upcoming Confederate offensive against the Union-held southern town.

Being a prisoner didn't surprise Rye. His destiny would be realized at the end of a noose. Twice before, Rye had escaped the hangman's rope. The first time in Pennsylvania when General Robert E. Lee, commander of the Army of Northern Virginia, needed information for a possible later mission. The second time in Virginia occurred mere weeks before he made his way to Tennessee.

It wasn't easy. The Union Soldiers had controlled Murfreesboro since early summer. When Rye arrived, he stayed with traitors, smugglers, and other spies almost forty miles away in Nashville. He fit right in with other males fighting in the regular army. The women would never turn him in because of their dislike of the Northern armies that occupied the region.

Rye stopped at the west fork of the Stones River, which marked the geographical center of the state of Tennessee.

"No one told you to stop, Confederate. Move."

Rye trudged through the water. The heavy chains tired him along with the continuous throbbing through his shoulder. He struggled across the river and glimpsed the outskirts of Murfreesboro. Union soldiers lined up along the street as the Confederate captain struggled to walk. A rock hit him on his sore shoulder. He squelched in the pain but continued to walk.

The soldiers spit and jeered at him. "Hang him right now. He's a Confedcrate."

A Union major stopped the men in front of the jail. "Where did you find him?"

The sergeant spoke up, "Hanging around in the trees outside of town."

The major turned back to Rye. "Who are you?"

Rye did not say anything, but his glare spooked the major. The two stared at each other.

"Throw him in with the other Confederate soldiers. He'll be hanged with the rest of them."

The gruff sergeant led Rye to the jail. Two soldiers joined him, their rifles pointed directly at his heart. For a moment, while the sergeant fumbled for the jail keys, Rye scanned the jail. Cobwebs adorned every corner and mustiness permeated the air. He peered back in the jail cell. Three Confederate soldiers with bones sticking out where flesh had been were staring at him with desperate eyes. Another captain sat on the floor. Other prisoners leaned against the walls.

The small jail looked secure, made of solid brick, so escape would be difficult. Three small bars allowed the prisoners to see the gallows outside the window, a ploy that always caused anxiety among those in the cell.

"Enjoy your short stay," the sergeant chuckled, slamming the door shut. "Sergeant Edward McDuffie's the name. You won't forget it."

Rye gazed out the window at the gallows. He imagined other Confederate soldiers' lives had ended with that noose for crimes they had not committed. On the day before his freedom, he vividly remembered one of the last few words the sergeant had said.

"Look away, Reb, or else I'll put this rifle butt against your face," the hefty Union sergeant said.

Captain Rye Tyler's icy stare sent a visible shiver through the sergeant.

"Tomorrow your neck will be stretched," the sergeant said. "I'll be there to see it. When it's done, I'll pluck those pretty blue eyes of yours and add them to my collection of Confederate body parts."

***

The sergeant turned and laughed, heading back toward the entrance of the jail. Confederate soldiers were housed in this place. Civilians were jailed in the courthouse.

McDuffie chuckled a little as he thought of the Union major. The sadistic son of a bitch hated rebels. He did too. No trial. No lawyers. No defense. Guilty. Death by hanging.

McDuffie enjoyed each and every verdict, even more because the major wouldn't hesitate to hang the dirty bastards.

Despite his dislike for all Confederate soldiers, Captain Tyler frightened him. If given the chance, that Confederate would rip out his throat or at least try. McDuffie would oblige the Confederate captain in a fight. His two-hundred-fifty pounds outweighed the Confederate captain by at least fifty to eighty pounds, and his six-foot-four-inch frame hovered at least two inches over him. He'd never met the man, but McDuffie had a job to do; one not associated with the Civil War. He'd killed the original McDuffie to find this man who landed right into his lap.

The sergeant turned around one more time and glanced into the jail cell. The captain's icy stare met his gaze.

"Come on, McDuffie, let's get a move on it. The major is getting kind of antsy," Private Smith said.

McDuffie, Smith, and another private, Campbell, stared at the prisoners in the jail. McDuffie finally left.

***

Once gone, Rye spoke to the other captain in the cell, "How long have you been in here?"

"At least two weeks," he said. "There's been no hope."

"There is hope," Rye said. "Forrest is coming. We just have to hold out another day or so."

Rye moved around the cell to check on the two wounded soldiers. "You're going to make it," he told them. "Even if I have to carry you on my back." He said this with confidence. Several times Rye had gone behind enemy lines to bring out soldiers who were captured. He received an award for valor twice. For his bravery, Confederate President Jefferson Davis appointed him a spy for the Confederate Army. Now after a year and a half working behind enemy lines, the dreaded death by hanging hovered over him.

All spies knew this could happen if captured. The other men in the cell with him didn't deserve death by hanging

4

from a sadistic Union major.

While others in the cell might have lost all hope, Rye would never admit defeat. His upbringing wouldn't allow that. No, a thousand troopers would arrive soon. Rye had too much information to help Forrest's mission to disrupt the federal supply lines in this area. He refused to die in a noose.

Rye figured the date to be July 12, 1862. He propped himself back up against the stone wall of the jail. In his mind, he reviewed every detail about Murfreesboro and the Union soldiers defending the depot. Murfreesboro consisted of a widely scattered and inefficiently led Union brigade, one camp west of town and another even farther west on the banks of Stones River.

The biggest problem involved the Union major. Rye had no illusions that he would kill all of them before he retreated. The major, a brutal killer and coward, would retreat. McDuffie worried him most. Something about him didn't add up. Rye drifted off to sleep but woke up with a start. The roar of an approaching storm grew louder and came nearer. "Wake up," he said. "Confederate soldiers are here."

The soldiers stirred. Rye hurried over to the young private. He'd died in his sleep. A bullet whizzed past Rye and hit the wall beside him. McDuffie started shooting at the prisoners. Rye pulled prisoners into a nook in a forward corner of the cell. McDuffie shot another wounded soldier, and blood splattered on Rye's shirt.

Rye gathered the others back into the corner as McDuffie and the other two started to scatter.

"Hold it, Smith," McDuffie said. "Light these papers. We'll burn the sons-of-a-bitches before we leave. That will show that cold-eyed captain who is the better soldier."

Rye couldn't see the fire but could smell the smoke. "They're going to burn us alive," one Confederate soldier screamed. He rushed toward the bars, screaming as the flames engulfed him. Rye couldn't do anything.

He went to the window and tried to pry the bars. No use.

He and others turned to hear someone prying the heavy metal door. The Confederate soldiers managed to bend it enough to rescue the remaining prisoners out of the burning building.

Rye looked at the other soldier on the ground. Dead. Good men died this morning, killed by a brutal Union sergeant and two privates. Rye should never forget their agonized faces. He then remembered Nathan Bedford Forrest sitting on his horse. The other captain in the cell considered him the epitome of a Confederate colonel. They had known each other throughout the war. Rye had heard of the man. At this point he really didn't give a damn about the man or the war. He couldn't get the defenseless prisoners' faces out of his mind. Rye became a deserter once he rode away from Murfreesboro. Let them come after him.

Chapter 1

August 17, 1862. Rye halted the Black and scanned the wide open land of Minnesota, which had become a state in 1858. The place of his birth. Now he didn't care about or remember anything about Minnesota. The trail of revenge led him to this state and to a place where he didn't know what to expect. All he knew was—he would not stop hunting down the three Union soldiers who massacred defenseless Confederate soldiers in a rotted jail.

Cottonwood trees and shrubs lined the Minnesota River bank. With his Sharps rifle ready to fire, Rye crawled off his black mustang horse, bent down, and used his left hand to cup cool water.

Rye had reached the massive Minnesota River Valley. Many considered Minnesota the western frontier and sparsely populated. The land consisted of rolling hills and green forests with a few farms and villages thrown in. The Sioux roamed the Minnesota River Valley from two main locations along the river—the upper Sioux Agency and the lower Sioux Agency.

A few miles back, Rye left New Ulm, heading west along the Cottonwood River. The trail led north to the Redwood River. He remembered a log cabin not far from where he stood. In that cabin, an evil man had raised at least two older brothers he knew of, an older and younger sister with manipulation and brutality. At ten, his father shipped Rye off to his aunt's in Tennessee. He never knew why.

Murfreesboro, Tennessee changed Rye's outlook on life. It made him hardened and bitter. Coming back to Minnesota wouldn't change his demeanor. He didn't care a whit.

The Dakota Sioux roamed the countryside in Minnesota. Staying alert meant staying alive. He hadn't seen an Indian or had any problems, but the people in New Ulm said the Indians were up to something. At least one old-timer he'd met on the trail a few miles past New Ulm talked of Indians being cheated by the United States Government, especially by some of the men who ran trading posts along the Minnesota River Indian reservations, which ran up and down the river in southwest Minnesota on fewer acres of land each year.

The old-timer also said the younger Sioux warriors talked about war and annihilation of the Whites. The Sioux leaders sold their land too cheaply to the White Eyes. Their leaders had also become White Eyes themselves. Many Sioux warriors despised their blood becoming farmers. They felt betrayed.

Rye filled his canteen, and after the mustang had quenched his thirst, Rye climbed back into the saddle. He continued west along the Cottonwood River, with a few miles to go before heading north. The trail had gone cold, but Rye believed the three men had come to Minnesota.

Rye had traveled from the mouth of the Cottonwood at New Ulm. The Cottonwood, a tributary of the Minnesota River, flowed into Minnesota just south of New Ulm. Rye followed the meandering river for at least ten miles. In those ten, he'd seen enough cottonwood trees to understand how the river received its name.

Those trees offered concealment from any Indian or others intent on ambushing anyone traveling along the river.

Rye pulled his slicker over his body. The wind picked up. He methodically followed the winding riverbank. The wind and rain made traveling slow going, draining the energy of both man and horse.

They traveled another mile before Rye spotted an area in which the two could find shelter from the rain and wind. He reined the horse to its left, and the mustang scrambled up a small embankment on the south side of the river. Rye went into a thicket of trees and brush, climbed off his horse, and quickly gathered some loose sticks to build a fire to warm up. After Rye started the fire, he took the saddle off of the mustang, then warmed his hands over the small fire.

Rye opened a bag of beans, dumped them into a pan, and fried them over the fire. He didn't feel hungry, but he needed to eat something.

Slowly finishing off the beans and drinking from the canteen, Rye settled down underneath a tree. The rain continued but had lost its strength. He had no plans to go anywhere, so he stretched out under his slicker.

The rain had almost come to a complete stop sometime while he was asleep. When he awoke later, his eyes landed on a pair of moccasins. A glimpse flashed of thinly shaped, bronze-copper legs, then an Indian dress, and ending with a woman with hazel eyes.

A branch snapped and the young woman disappeared into the brush. Sweat poured down Rye's face. Not from the humidity, but from the shock of seeing the copper-haired young girl.

Rye headed northwest toward the Redwood River. He kept thinking about the young woman. Why did she take off? Where did she go?

The black mustang brought Rye back to reality. The horse quickly stopped on the trail and pawed his hoofs. The Black smelled trouble. His horse had a knack for knowing danger. When the two-year-old started acting this way, Rye always prepared himself.

"Whoa, boy," he said calmly to the horse. "What is it?"

The horse didn't spook easily. Rye jumped off and pulled the horse back into the trees. A few minutes later, three white men emerged from the trees. One studied the ground and pointed toward Rye's location.

Were they looking for the young half-breed? Rye wondered. The mustang continued to be spooked. His horse didn't fear the smell of a white man. The three trackers continued upriver, and a few minutes later they disappeared. Rye led the horse out of the trees when an Indian showed up on the opposite bank. He studied the ground and looked up the river. Before he headed after the three men, he glanced toward Rye.

Rye didn't move until the Indian left. The Indian headed up the trail. Rye waited about ten more minutes before he walked the horse out of the trees and climbed aboard. He took a few minutes to survey the area and then continued his trek toward the northwest.

Rye arrived at a broken-down old cabin late in the afternoon. The shack sat on the north side of the Redwood River about a hundred feet back from the river. Close enough to quickly gather water, but far enough away to alleviate flooding that occurred each spring.

Weeds surrounded the one-room building. A closer glance showed one window had been broken and one hinge held the front door. It looked like three had been holding it together.

Rye climbed off his horse and slowly opened the door. He pushed aside the cobwebs hanging from the entrance and walked in. Once inside, Rye scanned the area. Cracked walls were his first impression, and a rocking chair stood in the middle of the room faded and broken.

He walked over to a desk against a wall. He noticed a family picture. Rye picked it up and looked at the torn photo. It looked like one or maybe even two people had been removed from the photo. He put it back down.

A creak on the floor caused him to whirl around, his pistol drawn. A woman stood there pointing a shotgun at him. Her light blue eyes glowed with the setting of the sun and showed her tanned, healthy skin. A loose, button-down shirt with jeans fit her body nicely. Rye stood six-foot-two. He figured this woman stood five-nine-inches tall.

***

Before she spoke, the woman noticed his long, dark hair down to his shoulders and the growth of hair around his face. His dark blue eyes made her heart skip. It could only be Rye. Those eyes gave him away. She would never forget those midnight blue eyes. He'd grown into a handsome man, even with the scruffy dark hair and beard. The man was solidly built, nothing like his brothers. "Who are you?"

***

Rye didn't say anything.

Someone else stepped in behind her with a rifle. He had eyes colored like a grizzly bear. "Looks like a no-good. Maybe we should just shoot him. What do you think, Ubel?"

"Naw," said another man who appeared behind him. Right after them two young women emerged. The younger girl had a curvaceous body and almond-shaped eyes that said self-righteous woman. The older one was plain-faced and a little stubbier.

The second man pointed his gun at Rye. "You'd better drop your weapon, mister. You are trespassing, and we could just as well shoot you now."

Rye slowly unbuckled his gun belt and dropped it on the floor. The man called Ubel reached down and picked the gun belt up. He motioned for Rye to sit on the floor in the corner.

"I'm hungry," Ubel said. "How about you ladies fix up some grub, and we'll all sit down and have a long chat with our guest. Maybe he knows something about what is happening around here."

One of the women spoke up, "There is nothing here to eat. This cabin has been empty for days. We're just here to make sure we didn't miss anything. You know what Libbie's father would say if we did."

Rye's eyes traveled to the taller woman. Libbie Davis. He would never forget her face and her eyes. Libbie had reddish-brown hair, probably bronzed from the sun. He knew her immediately when the young woman walked through the door with the shotgun pointed at him. Rye studied the cluster of people who'd walked in. The first woman had a different approach to life than the others. The rest possibly had lived in this cabin at one time. The man called Ubel had a corpse-like skin and age spots on his face. He looked to be in his forties.

The other called Armstrong had a birthmark showing on his neck and eyes colored like a grizzly bear.

As far as the women, the older woman had ash blond colored hair with fair, dull eyes. The other girl had soft smooth skin with almond-shaped eyes.

"Hey, mister?" The man called Armstrong brought him back to the present. "Why are you here?"

Rye thought about his answer. "I needed rest, found this place, and wanted to find a place to sleep other than the hard ground."

"That makes sense, Armstrong," Ubel said. "I wouldn't want to sleep on the ground either."

A real winner, Rye thought.

"Where are you from?"

Again, Rye thought about his answer. "I came from the West," he lied. "from Dakota Territory."

"Indians too much for you out there?" Ubel said grinning with a tooth missing.

"Yeah. That's right. He doesn't look like a man that could handle a little trouble."

Ubel glanced once more at Rye. "You might as well stay here. Ain't anyone else going to be here."

**

When he had turned away, the taller woman snuck a quick glance at his sun-browned features and penetrating blue eyes. Rye Tyler seemed to be like no man she had ever known. The man didn't seem like the same twelve-year-old boy.

With Rye here, this only meant trouble. Her father would find out sooner or later. She wouldn't be the one to tell him. Libbie Davis would never say anything to harm the man she had loved all twenty years of her life. Rye would die immediately if her father found out. She hoped her emotions would not give him away. Libbie knelt down on one knee, looking at Rye. "Who are you?" she asked, knowing she couldn't or wouldn't let on that she knew exactly who he was.

He smiled at her. She sensed he didn't smile much.

"Libbie, why are you there with him?" Armstrong asked, who had stepped over to the corner of the cabin, breaking the silence. "I don't want you messing around with any other man. You're my woman and no one else looks at you."

***

"Oh, I see. I'm sorry," Rye said, piercing her with his gaze. Only Libbie could break his heart. It was happening now. Rye told himself it shouldn't matter. Libbie couldn't be in his life because Rye had dangerous things to attend to. He'd never put her in harm's way.

"Please, it isn't what he says," Libbie said. Too late. Rye turned away. "Why did you do that? You have no right to claim me."

"Now, Libbie, your father and mother want us to be hitched."

"Then you go marry my mother and my father." Libbie stomped out of the cabin.

***

She couldn't stand the man. In fact, she couldn't stand any of the Tyler family, but they scared her. This so-called plan terrified her. The Tyler family members had no clue of the plan to become rich at the expense of the Sioux nation. They were afraid of Rye. Her father would eliminate him if he ever found the man. Libbie would do her best to make sure that they would never find out he had sat in a corner in this cabin. It had been ten years since Rye disappeared.

She'd not seen him since then. Every time she thought of him, her heart fluttered. It broke her heart to be part of a plan that could eventually destroy Rye, but she had no choice.

***

Rye sensed the hostility in the room. He wanted to be anywhere but here. But he'd continue his quest and wouldn't let anyone know about it.

"Hey, mister. You wanted to know what happened to the man and lady out there? Well, I'll tell you," the man called Ubel said. "They're dead." He uttered an evil laugh.

"Ubel, they have only been in the ground a couple days. At least give them a few days before you act like an idiot," the woman called Lorelei said.

"I'm not an idiot," he spat out.

"She's just kidding," Rikka said smiling sweetly. She turned to Rye. "The thieving Indian, Otaktay, killed him for no reason. At least three arrows in his chest and his left hand missing. A pretty gory sight. I almost got sick, but I held it together. As for Mother, once she heard about it, she just got up and died – a heart attack, I think. That's about the extent of it."

Rye looked around the room. Everyone but Libbie seemed satisfied it happened as she explained. He'd talk to her and find out how it really happened when he could get her alone. Until then, he'd just bide his time. So, he sat in the corner listening to them telling their sickening stories and laughing at jokes that weren't even funny. Rye had no idea who these people were, but he was too tired to figure it out.

Chapter 2

Tender hands shook Rye awake. Libbie. Rye smiled at her. She smiled back.

"Who are you?" she asked.

"A drifter."

"I'll head back to the fort. Please stay away," she whispered and turned to leave.

Rye looked after Libbie who raced out the door.

"Hurry up, Libbie, or we'll be late for our meeting," Lorelei said.

***

Libbie glanced one last time at Rye, then hurried up the path to join the others. No one else said a word to Rye. Libbie's heart couldn't stop racing after seeing him for the first time in many years. His stature, his smile—those she remembered. He looked beaten down and angry. She had to do something to save him but didn't know what she could do. Libbie's fear of the men associated with her family put a strangle hold on her, and the Sioux kept her in check. She had seen them torture and kill men because they didn't comply. And several of the men doing those atrocities were her brothers and Rye's as well. One such brother Libbie had never seen but had heard about him. Someday he and Rye would meet. It terrified her what would happen to Rye when they did.

***

After they left, Rye looked around the cabin. This would

be his home for a short period of time. Rye attached the door back on homemade hinges, so it closed properly. It took him most of the morning to do that. After the door was secure, Rye pulled food out of his pack. After finishing the meal, he used his knife to remove the hair on his face. He also used his knife to cut the long locks off the back of his head. The hair barely touched his neck. He felt much better.

Rye peered into a cracked mirror and saw a man on a mission. He had always been shy but couldn't remember its source. For some reason he had never felt shy around Libbie Davis. He would never reveal himself to her. Rye did not want to be the reason for her destruction. He needed to forget her.

He never understood why he had been shipped to Tennessee. But once the Civil War broke out, Rye knew that he needed to fight for the Confederacy. He believed that everyone should have the right to do as they chose. Rye grew up with slaves. As a youngster, he had no friends except the slaves; the kindest people he had ever met. God-fearing people. Rye never really understood the Bible. He remembered reading parts of it one time or another. He also remembered hearing others read words out of it on occasion. The Bible would not be something for him. The book wouldn't want a killer like Rye Tyler had turned into.

Growing up in Tennessee seemed so long ago. He had one goal. Find the men who slaughtered innocent men in a confined jail. But as a deserter, he'd be hanged on sight if caught by the Northern Army.

He looked away from the mirror and came back to the present.

After lunch he rode to the trader's post to gather necessities for his stay at the cabin. Once on the horse, the mustang took off. He sniffed. Smoke everywhere.

An hour later he came upon a trading post, or the remains of a trading post. He glanced around. There had been a warehouse, stores, and different types of houses.

Portions of a steam sawmill toward the back. He stopped his horse in front of the trader's post and checked around the buildings.

Dead bodies lay around the yard. Rye noticed a man dead on the opposite side of the building. It looked like he jumped out of a second-story window to escape. He didn't get too far. Rye looked down at the man. Grass filled his mouth. Rye looked around a few moments more. Nothing he could do here. He didn't bury them because he knew Sioux were still running around looking for other whites. A war had started in Minnesota.

It had taken him an hour to make the three-mile trek to the trading post, but he took some different routes in order to lose anybody that might be following him. He rode slowly through the trees. For some reason, it seemed like he knew where all the trails led. He couldn't understand it. It had been eleven years since he'd been in Minnesota.

As he came out of a grove of trees, he heard screaming off to his left. Rye stopped. Three men struggled with someone on the ground. He couldn't determine who they had. He slowly walked the horse back to the grove of trees and crept toward the sound. A few minutes later he saw the men. They had a young girl down on the ground.

"Let her go," he said.

As a group, they spun around. "Like hell," one of them said.

Rye put a single shot into the group. They jumped back. Rye, with his pistol aimed at them, approached the young girl. She quickly covered her breasts with her hands and the ragged shirt they tore off. The young half-breed girl who had spooked him yesterday. She didn't have a tear on her face.

"Now, come on, mister. Let us have some fun with the breed. You can tell she is young and needs our type of loving."

"Just walk that way," Rye said pointing toward the north. "Now, or the next shot will not miss."

One started to say something. Rye put a slug into his shoulder.

"Damn, you busted my shoulder up," he squealed.

"If you don't move away from here, it will be your other shoulder, then a leg—"

The man whirled around and ran toward the trees. The others hurried after him heading toward the north.

After they were out of sight, Rye reached down and took the young girl's hand, pulling her up from the ground. He brushed grass out of her hair and off the back of her shirt. "I will not harm you," he said.

"I know. I am not afraid of you."

"Here, let me help you." Her shoulder had been raked across with what looked like fingernails. She covered her breasts. Rye whistled for the mustang. Once the black horse came, Rye grabbed a blanket off the horse and wrapped the young girl in it. "Where are your people?"

"My mother lives on the reservation. I do not know where my Indian father is."

"What are you doing out here?"

The young girl did not answer.

"I will take you to a cabin to doctor up that shoulder. It is close by."

The young girl smiled.

"What are you smiling about?" Again, she did not answer. Rye helped her up onto the horse and then crawled up behind her heading the horse toward the cabin. Once in the saddle, the horse quickened its step, sensing that trouble could be coming any time. Rye made it back to the cabin at suppertime. He helped the young girl down and walked her into the cabin. "Here, sit down on the rocker. Let me get something to put on that wound."

The young girl studied him closely. Rye had a feeling that this woman would bring trouble. Tall for a half-breed; at least five or six inches shorter than his tall frame. He searched around the house for some clothes for the woman to wear, finding a skirt and blouse that he figured his sister, Rikka, had worn. He hoped the clothes would fit the half-breed. "Here you can put these on. These clothes might be a bit too small, but they are a lot better than what you are wearing."

"Your woman's clothes?" she asked.

"No, a woman named Rikka has worn them. She wouldn't mind you wearing the clothes until I can take you back to your mother." Rye was searching for salve to soothe her shoulder when something rustled behind him. He twisted around. The young girl stood naked but quickly slipped on the skirt Rye had given her. It fit her almost perfectly.

"I'm sorry. You could have dressed in the other room."

"I am done now," she said. "You can turn back around. I am not ashamed that you saw my body."

"What do you mean?" Rye asked as he applied ointment on the girl's shoulder. "I am a half-breed. My mother is Sioux and my father is your kind. The Sioux custom is for me to stay with you because you have saved me. But, as I am your kind also, I understand that if you do not want me, I will go."

"At this point, I do not think you would want me," Rye exclaimed.

She didn't answer.

"How about I just fix you up and take you back to your family?"

"That would be fine...for now," Rye glanced up at her last two words. "What is your name?"

"I am Mina. What is your name?"

"They call me Rye Tyler."

"Rye Tyler. I will remember that name. You were the man in the bushes a few days ago."

"Yes. What were you doing out there?"

"I like to wander."

Rye looked at her. "What do you mean?"

She didn't answer back. The young girl went into the

other bedroom and crawled into bed.

Rye could not sleep. He had to think. Before he knew it, the sun had risen in the sky. Rye didn't know if he'd gotten any sleep at all.

A voice hollered from outside the cabin. "Hey, mister, let us have the half-breed bitch, and we won't burn the cabin down," the man said.

Rye woke with a start, grabbed his rifle, and opened the door with the rifle pointing toward them.

Ubel stood there, smiling. "Oh, you are still here. We want the girl. We have to finish something."

"I can't do that. She is here of her own free will."

Another man spoke up. "Come on, Ubel, maybe he wants some of that half-breed body for himself. Or maybe he wouldn't know what to do with something that pretty."

Rye recognized the third man immediately – one of the guards at the Murfreesboro jail. The guard finally spoke up, "You can just shoot him because he escaped from a Tennessee jail."

The other two swung around. "You don't say," Ubel said, turning back to face Rye. He palmed his pistol but must have thought better of pulling the trigger after the click of Rye's rifle aimed squarely at him got his attention.

"You can go away now. I'm a dead shot, and this bullet will kill you before you move, with more shots and time to spare for your friends here."

"You can't kill us all," the jailer said.

Rye stared to the north, not saying a word. Then, in a measured tone, he said, "No, but I will kill you before I go. That I am sure of. And if you all weren't so set on harming a young, innocent woman, you would have noticed all the smoke in the valley. Maybe her family is coming for you and burning everything in sight."

"Don't fill us with those lies. Her family is on the reservation."

They spun in the direction Rye had indicated. Rye said,

"I just came from one of the trading posts. All dead. In fact, one man had grass stuck in his mouth."

The men peered at each other. "Oh my God, that must be Myrick. He refused to give the Sioux credit one time, and I heard the man tell the Sioux to let them eat grass. We'd better get out of here."

The jailer fidgeted. "Maybe we'd better head back to town. I don't like it that the Sioux might be on the warpath."

Ubel whipped around and glared at the man. "Another person scared of his own shadow? Let's go back." He turned but stopped at the path. "The next time you won't be as fortunate, mister."

"Hey, you, next time you come, make sure you bring plenty of people to help you. You'll need it." Rye turned his back and strode into the cabin.

Mina came up to him and quickly kissed him on the cheek. "Thanks."

Rye felt the warmth on his face from the kiss.

"No problem. What worries me is the smoke. Are the Sioux going on the warpath?"

"Yes," she said. "They are hungry. They are angry. They will kill all the whites."

"What about you?"

"I will be okay. Otaktay is my brother. He will not let anything happen to me."

"I had better get you back to your parents." Rye had managed to reach the river when a ghastly scream made him peer up. Running feet clamored toward the cabin. He grabbed his rifle and scrambled back up the path toward it. Rye quickly opened the door and bolted it from the inside.

"What is it?"

"I don't know, Mina. I heard a scream and then running feet coming this way."

Screams from outside sounded close. He inched the door open. Two white men raced out of the clearing and ran for the cabin. At first glance, Rye counted at least ten painted warriors chasing them.

"Open up, Mister. Please open up."

Mina rested her hand on Rye's shoulder. "Do not open that door. If you let them in, the Sioux will kill you."

"I can't just let them die." He swung open the door and fired two quick shots into the ground in front of the Indians who stopped in the path. It provided enough time for the two white men to hurry into the cabin—Ubel and one of the privates at Murfreesboro.

"Thanks. I knew we would be safe here."

"You are not safe here," Mina spoke up. "Not only will they kill you, you have also signed this man's death warrant because he has helped you."

Ubel turned with a smirk on his lips.

Chapter 3

The leader of the warriors hollered at the cabin, "Come, let us take you to safety. My brothers have gone to war and are killing whites in the area. If you are with us, you will be safe."

Rye opened the door a crack. He stepped out. "Go away. I have not harmed any of you. I just want to live in peace in this cabin."

"This is the Tyler cabin. It will be burned to the ground and all the people in it for the evil deeds that the Tylers have done to the Sioux nation."

"I do not know what you are talking about. I have been away fighting in the big war between our brothers. How could I have done anything to your people?"

Momentary silence. "Then, you have nothing to fear by going with us to safety."

"I will not leave with you."

"Then you shall die with the rest of the whites in the valley." With that, the Sioux warriors ran into the trees.

"What do you think, mister?" the man asked.

"You're asking me? Tell me what happened that would make these Indians so upset?"

Silence in the room.

"I will tell you, but you will not like it," said Mina.

"Shut up, you whore," Ubel said.

Rye punched him and knocked him into the corner of the cabin. "It's time you shut your mouth. I want to hear what is happening around here. Go ahead, Mina, explain."

Mina explained to Rye what had been going on around the valley. She told him that Richard Tyler, along with many other families including the Davises, had been charging the Sioux high prices for all their purchases. If the Sioux couldn't pay, then the whites would extend credit for the items they needed. Many were those needed to survive. When the annuities came in, then the white store owners would keep all the money. The Indians always had to start over. They also take advantage of the Indian women," she said. "I am half white, so they do not hurt me until today. This man and these others do not like me and would like to kill me."

"You got that right," said the Murfreesboro private. "If it wasn't for your Indian lover friend here, we would have taken care of you. We still might."

"No, you won't," said Rye, shifting the rifle toward him. "You make one move toward her, and I will pull this trigger. Survival is my main concern. Right now, I could pull this trigger for what you did at Murfreesboro. But, I won't because I need you to fight. If you survive, I will kill you."

The former private's face turned red. He looked at Ubel.

Who is this man?" Ubel asked turning to the Murfreesboro private. "You said you knew him."

"I only know him as a Confederate spy who is sentenced to die by hanging."

Ubel looked at the man. "Mister, if the Indians don't kill you, I will. I despise Confederate soldiers, particularly spies."

The screaming brought everyone in the cabin back to the present. Indians sprinted out of the woods firing muskets, shooting bows and arrows, and throwing tomahawks at the cabin. Rye and the two other white men ducked under open windows and fired. The number increased from the ten initial Sioux during the attack. Rye lifted his rifle, fired, and knocked one of the lead warriors to the ground. The Indian didn't move. The other two fired behind him but missed the mark.

Rye handed the rifle to Mina who loaded it for him. He turned and continued firing with his pistol. He then handed her the pistol. Mina had taken Rye's gun belt off his hips during the fight.

After the first wave, the Sioux retreated into the trees.

"You're a pretty good shot," Ubel said, wiping powder from his face. "Guess the Confederate boys taught you a thing or two about firing a weapon."

Rye didn't say anything. He glanced at the jailer who stood shaking. Rye shook his head. That explained why only three Indians had died.

Before Rye could say anything, the Indians raced out of the woods once more. This time they used fire arrows to burn the cabin. The arrows did not catch fire to the roof because of an earlier rain that had left it wet. A few arrows stuck on the north side setting that portion of the cabin on fire.

"Put the fire out or they will burn us out," Rye said.

Mina grabbed a blanket and beat the fire with it. Rye and Ubel continued to fire at the Sioux, while the jailer huddled in the corner.

Ubel yelled at him, "If you're not going to fire your weapon, at least help the half-breed bitch put the fire out."

He crawled to his feet and grabbed a bucket for water. Within minutes the two had the fire out. Again, the Indians ceased attacking and disappeared into the woods.

"You think they will come back, mister?" Ubel asked.

"How would I know?" He looked over at Mina. "Are you okay?"

"Yes, I'm fine. I do not believe the Sioux will attack again for now. They have lost too many warriors. They will never forgive you."

Rye didn't say anything. He looked out the window. He counted five dead Indians. There could be more back in the trees. He kept his focus on the trees, while at the same time glancing back at the two in the cabin. Whatever they did next, he'd be ready.

As for Mina, she stayed behind Rye and out of the sights of the two in the cabin. That woman had strength. She could be deadly.

An hour later Rye opened the door and inched out. The other men followed him.

"I guess we'll head back toward Fort Ridgely. It looks like the redskins have left."

"Hold it," Rye said.

They stopped in their tracks. The two men turned slowly around and looked at Rye.

"I want that man," said Rye, nodding toward the man from Murfreesboro. Ubel glanced at Rye and then at the man from Murfreesboro.

"Who are you, mister?" he asked once more.

Rye nodded toward the man. "This is our fight."

Ubel frowned at him. "You want to fight a white man in the middle of an Indian War? What is wrong with you? Are you crazy?"

"He is a murderer."

"And you are a traitor and a spy," the man said, charging toward Rye with a knife.

Rye dodged to the left as the man tripped over the corner of the steps. He kicked Smith in the mouth with his foot. The man rolled over, and Rye climbed on top of him. Smith clawed for his knife, but Rye lifted him up and pounded on him with his fists. One to the jaw, another to the stomach, and a third punch back to the jaw. The dazed man stumbled over the porch. Rye picked him up again and slapped him hard.

The man huddled covering his head with his hands to protect him from the onslaught. Sniffing back tears, he said, "Butler Lily made me do it," he said and looked up through pleading eyes.

That stopped Rye. "Butler Lily. Who is he?"

"Sergeant McDuffie at the jail. He isn't really a sergeant. And that's not his real name. They sent him to kill you."

"Why would he want to kill me? Who are they?"

"That I can't answer."

Rye spun around and strode toward the porch. The man saw his chance, grabbed the knife, and started toward him. Rye pulled his pistol from his holster, twisted around, and put a bullet in the man's forehead killing him instantly. "One down, two to go," he said to himself.

Ubel stared in shock, then strode toward the road.

"Aren't you going to take your friend with you?"

"You killed him. You bury him," Ubel said.

Rye shook his head and waved him off.

"He will not make it to the fort," Mina said. "The Sioux will be waiting for him and will kill him. Then they will come here."

"We'd better get out of here. I'll bury him first. Everyone deserves that."

Rye grabbed a shovel and dragged Smith around back. An hour later he finished the job. Rye went inside, checked his rifle, and headed back toward the window. Fires burned to the north. Would Ubel make it to Fort Ridgely? He doubted it. Why did he even care? They didn't care a hoot about him.

Within ten minutes, Mina came over to the window with what looked like soup.

"What is it?"

"It is an Indian dish. I hope you like it."

He took a sip. "It tastes good," he said. He was almost finished when a voice came from the trees.

"Hey, you in the cabin. We have something for you."

Rye opened the door a crack and stuck his rifle out before stepping out. Lying on the porch was a severed hand. "Don't look," Rye told Mina. "It's a hand."

The girl froze. "Otaktay," she said.

"Who is he? Was Otaktay with the earlier group?" Rye asked.

"I did not see. But, I do not think so. He travels on his own. He is called a lone wolf…like you."

"This man is dead," the voice said again from the shadows.

"Show your face. Who are you?"

"I am called Otaktay. I have sworn to kill the Tyler family and anyone associated with them for what they have done to our people." The lone warrior stepped out of the trees. Pox marks covered his face. Rye stepped out of the door to face him.

"There needs to be no fighting between us, Otaktay. I've not done anything to harm your people."

"You stay in the Tyler cabin. He destroyed many Sioux. You die with other whites who hurt Sioux. I kill all. I do not want my half-sister to die with you. I will take her away from here."

"You had better go, Mina. You will be much safer with him. If they attack this place, you could get killed."

Mina approached Otaktay. She turned around to look at Rye, then joined Otaktay. The two walked toward the smoke.

Chapter 4

Price Davis raised a gnarled hand to his lips and glanced at his family gathered around his home just outside of Fort Ridgely. With the river valley up in smoke, it would be only a matter of time before the Sioux warriors attacked the fort. Before the Sioux attacked, the Davis family could walk a dozen steps and be within the safe confines of the fort.

The fort would be hard to overtake because of the ravines surrounding it. Fort Ridgely also had the distinction of being one of the highest points in the area. Word had come back earlier in the day that Captain Marsh and most of his company had been killed near the Redwood Ferry. Those who survived and made it to the fort told of atrocities throughout the valley. Price Davis didn't know what to think. He'd heard stories of Indian attacks over the past ten years. None had materialized. But for some reason, he believed the stories this time. Davis had helped instigate the Sioux uprising. It didn't faze him. His money was safe in a Minnesota bank. He could just pack up his family and move elsewhere.

The Sioux were stupid, he thought. The Indian people didn't understand the white man's strength and their desire to rule. He always made sure when any annuities came in from the federal government, he charged more than he should, in order to keep the Sioux in their needy place. The deceit kept the Indians in check.

He looked out his window. Men, women, and children continued to pour into the fort. Throughout the day, Davis estimated that at least two-hundred-fifty people had arrived seeking safety. Gere had done what he could. He put the women and children in the large stone barracks building. Established a defensive perimeter around the post using wagons, barrels, and anything useful for defense.

Even with all the movement from the countryside, Davis still hadn't figured out for sure if the Sioux had torched or killed in the territory. It didn't matter to him as long as it didn't get in the way of his business endeavor. Others would call it thievery. Everything had worked to Price Davis's satisfaction. But there was one obstacle. One man could destroy everything. Captain Rye Tyler in Tennessee. Butler Lily had failed to kill Tyler. Nobody knew where he had disappeared to. For that matter, no one knew what he looked like.

The man in Tennessee couldn't handle the job, but at this point it didn't matter. If the Sioux were ravaging the region, they'd kill everyone throughout the Minnesota River Valley.

"Price, are you in the parlor?"

He turned toward the voice, to his lovely wife. "Yes, dear, come on in. What is it you want?"

"I just came in to let you know supper is ready."

Price Davis glanced at the clock on the wall which said almost six. "I'll be right out."

Mrs. Davis didn't move. His wife had something on her mind. She also knew better than to interrupt her husband while working.

He turned to his wife. "What is it?"

"It is Libbie. I can't figure her out. The Tyler girls mentioned seeing a young man at their cabin. I could see a change in Libbie's demeanor when the girls talked about the man. She cares about that Tyler boy."

"That's not good. Talk to Blanche and put our next

phase into action."

"Blanche isn't here."

He stared at her. "Where did she go?"

"She took a ride with one of the men at the fort."

"With the valley going up in smoke? I swear. She's not like anyone in our family,"

"You know Blanche."

"Yeah, I do. Let's eat and see what transpires."

"Why would you think Blanche would be a solution to this Tyler kid? And what is it that you fear about him?"

"Rye Tyler has never met Blanche. He knows Libbie, but the hope is he's forgotten her, though it doesn't sound like she's forgotten him. As for your second question, the younger Tyler is a war hero. People know his name, and they will protect him. That is unless we can show who he really is."

"And what is that, dear?"

"A brutal murderer who has no conscience."

"That I can't understand either, but I trust your judgment." The two walked out for supper.

***

Rye gathered his gear. He couldn't go to Fort Ridgely. They would hang him. He couldn't hold off the Sioux by himself. Rye swung his rifle around at the sound of a branch snapping.

"Please, mister, don't shoot us," said a young girl who couldn't be more than sixteen or seventeen years old. Behind her stood a young boy and a young girl.

"Where is your family?"

"I'm Christina, and this is Jeremiah and Isabelle," The youngest girl's eyes welled with tears and she scrubbed her fist over her wet cheek. "They're all dead," Christina said. "The Indians killed them all."

The boy's head tilted, and he stared at Rye. "You are the only white man who stayed. Everyone else has runned."

Rye bolted the door after he ushered the three into the

cabin. The youngest girl wouldn't let him go. He looked at the young kids and couldn't believe they had survived a trek through Sioux country.

"My father, mother, and brothers died at the hands of the stinkin' Indians."

The oldest girl, Christina, scolded him. "Ma wouldn't like you talking like that about anyone, Jeremiah."

"They are stinkin' Indians. We have no family, sis. They're all dead."

"We still have each other. You don't know for sure if they're dead. There is still hope," Christina said. She then turned to Rye. "Someone mentioned this cabin, that a man may be here who would save us."

"How far did you walk?" Rye asked.

"Maybe four or five miles," Christina said.

"You didn't see any Indians?"

"No, not until we heard the shots close to the cabin."

"I bet you're hungry," said Rye, turning to get the soup.

"I'm really hungry," Jeremiah said. Christina walked over to help Rye. Isabelle remained attached to Rye's side.

"She must like you," Christina said. "Usually, she stays away from anyone she doesn't know."

Isabelle continued to hold on to Rye's hand and looked up at him through a tearful smile.

"It will be okay," Rye said.

The young girl said nothing. "Here, you'd better eat something. I won't be too far away." Rye took the girl's hand and led her to the table. She let go of his hand, jumped up into his arms, and circled his neck.

Rye held her for a few moments, not sure what to do. She finally stopped crying and he set her down in a chair at the table. He returned to the door, but Isabelle crawled out of the chair and ran after him.

"I am not going anywhere," he told her. "I will either be in the cabin or right outside the door. You are safe now." He took her hand and walked back with her to the chair. The other two children gobbled their soup down. Isabelle took a spoonful, then looked in Rye's direction after each bite. Rye opened the door and walked outside.

Instantly, Isabelle jumped out of the chair and scrambled after him, grabbing his hand. Rye glanced down at her.

"Okay, you win. You can stay with me, but you have to be very quiet and listen to everything I tell you."

The two walked around the cabin down to the river. Rye reached down to fill up the two pouches he had brought down for water. The young girl put her hand into the water and pulled it out quickly.

"It is cold," she said.

"Yes, it is cold. How old are you?"

"I will be eleven soon."

Rye quickly pushed the girl behind him, grabbed his pistol, and turned toward the grove of trees to his left.

Otaktay stared at them.

"What do you want, Otaktay?" Rye asked.

"White man, I see you are still alive."

"Where are the rest of your warriors?'

"I come alone. I am a lone wolf."

The young girl poked her head around Rye's shoulder. She did not pull on him, so Rye assumed that this Sioux warrior did not kill her family.

"What do you want?"

"You."

Rye said nothing at first, then, "You will find it harder to kill me than the others. What if I kill you first?"

Otaktay glared at the white man. "That will not happen."

"A bullet right between your two eyes will take care of that."

The Indian turned and disappeared into the grove of trees. Rye gathered the water, grabbed Isabelle's hand, and hurried back to the cabin. Before they went inside, Rye stopped and peered at the little girl.

"Do not say anything to anyone about this incident."

The little girl nodded.

The two stepped into the cabin. Christina rushed to her little sister's side. "Don't run off like that again."

The little girl nodded. "I am scared, Christina."

Christina took Isabelle's hand, led her to the bed in the other room, and climbed in beside her. Jeremiah sat down in a chair, and within minutes all three children were asleep.

Chapter 5

Rye didn't have a choice. He'd find a safe place for the three young children. They didn't deserve this. Against his better judgment, Rye would take them to Fort Ridgely in the morning. With this last thought, he fell asleep on the floor in the corner.

It was still dark when two little hands rubbed his arm. Rye scrubbed his eyes and looked at the girl named Isabelle. "You are an early bird, young lady," he said.

She smiled.

"Can you wake your brother and sister up? I'm going to take you to Fort Ridgely." Rye placed the saddle and bridle on the mustang, whispering in his ear to protect them.

Jeremiah asked, "why did you do that?"

"I wanted him to understand we are in danger."

Within an hour the little group started down a back trail that looked as if it had not been traveled for some time. Christina led the way. Jeremy brought up the rear. They heard screams and shots along the trail. The skies were hazy with fire and smelled of smoke.

By late morning they reached the Minnesota River. Rye felt the best thing to do would be to follow the river to the fort.

Christina touched his shoulder pointing toward a grove of trees.

"We'll be safe once we reach the trees," Rye said. He stopped and motioned for the others to get down. Indians rushed out of the brush. Rye snapped a shot, killing the first Indian who appeared. A second shot plugged the next Indian. A third shot killed an Indian just as he lifted his arm to bury a knife into Christina. Rye shot the Indian from the hip and then turned to face two others. He killed one. The other turned and ran back into the brush. "We'd better find a place to hide," Rye said. "He'll be back with others."

He waded into the river carrying Isabelle over his shoulders. The other two followed him. They made it across to the other side and rushed into the trees. Rye moved the children as quietly as possible knowing that any sound could mean their doom. Ten minutes later, more screams reached their ears.

"They've found our trail," he said. "We have to find a place to hide ourselves or we won't last long." Rye halted them for a moment. He looked at the children. "Our best bet is to go into the river and hide underneath some brush. Can you swim?"

They nodded and followed him to a brushy area on the south side of the river.

He quickly made reed straws so they could breathe underneath the water. He finished the first one for Christina and explained to her what to do. Then he told her to help others with their reeds once underneath the water.

Once he had them finished, including one for himself, he checked out the trail. He traveled about a hundred feet into a brush near a ridge. Rye dropped to the ground at the sound of rustling. Two warriors came up the trail he would have crossed. Another step and they would have found him. He waited for a few moments. When the Sioux warriors left, Rye waded back to the children.

He floated underneath the water and took the reed from Christina. He put it into his mouth and settled down with the children. A steady pattering of rain started. The rain would erase any of the tracks they had made. The small group would have to wait it out. Within half an hour, the rain finally subsided. Rye climbed out of the water and pulled Christina up after him. "It is safe to get back on the path. The Sioux will have a hard time finding our trail after the hard rain of the last hour. We'll still need to be as quiet as possible."

She nodded.

He slowly climbed out of the water onto the hill beside the river. Rye stopped for a moment and checked the area. Once he felt they were safe, he motioned for Jeremiah and helped him up the ledge. Jeremiah would have a better chance to shoot any Indians than the girls would.

"Quietly walk toward the river," he told him. Next Rye took Christina's hands and pulled her up to him. He gently helped her onto the ledge. He brought Isabelle up last. She put her arms around him. "Hold onto me tightly," Rye told her. Isabelle wasn't going to let go. He crawled up the ledge with her holding onto him.

The foursome trekked toward the fort. Humidity from the rain soaked their clothing. A grove of trees helped conceal their travels. They walked about thirty minutes before they came to a clearing.

Rye stopped suddenly and put his finger to his lips. The others stopped. Nobody moved. Six white men emerged from the clearing. Rye noticed a movement off to his left. An arrow whistled toward the group. One man screeched, clutching his throat.

Screeching warriors raced out of the trees. The small band ducked behind the available cover of bushes and fired at the Indians. Another group of Sioux came from the right, sandwiching the small party. None of the Indians appeared to have seen Rye and the children.

"They will be massacred if we don't do something," Rye whispered. "Please stay here out of sight. I'll give the Sioux something to think about."

He lay on the wet ground behind a log and aimed his rifle. He felt the rifle buck against his shoulder. The Indian screamed and fell backward. Rye got off a second shot. The warriors didn't see it coming and glanced around the area. During the lull in the fight, another shot took a brave to his death. The sound came from Jeremiah's direction.

Rye swore to himself, then smiled. The warriors were in a crossfire and at least six lay dead on the ground. The remaining Sioux bolted back into the trees.

"Thanks whoever you are," one of the men hollered from the trees. He stepped out with three others. Rye kept his rifle trained on the men. The leader stopped. He looked at Rye. A familiar face. Clayton Campbell, one of the guards in Murfreesboro.

"Well, it looks like the family is all together once more," Campbell said.

"Not everyone. You left a few behind," Rye said. His finger rested on the trigger. He could kill them all before they knew what happened, but he didn't want to do that.

Campbell smiled and put his pistol back in his holster. The others followed suit. "It isn't too far to the fort," he said.

"Campbell."

The Murfreesboro killer stopped and slowly turned to face Rye.

"There will be another time."

"I look forward to it," Campbell said. He strode away. The others in his party scurried behind him. Rye and the children followed behind. Christina led the Black.

Fort Ridgely sat on a hundred-fifty-foot bluff overlooking the Minnesota River. The fort sat exposed with no stockade around it. Each detached building could be seen from a distance. Less than a mile away was the river. One, maybe two houses, sat on a plateau to the north of the fort. To the northwest, open prairies. To the cast, northeast, and southwest, ravines. The main buildings circled a parade ground. On the northside sat a two-story stone barracks and another building.

Rye noticed a sutler's home, a warehouse, a store, and

what looked like two other buildings. Even further back stood large stables with haystacks alongside them

A lot of activity was going on around the parade grounds. For the survivors to get to the fort, they would have to climb up the hill out of one of the ravines from the southwest. The young ones struggled to get up the ravine, but after ten minutes, the small group stepped up to the fort.

"Hey, don't shoot. We're white settlers coming in," Clayton Campbell hollered.

A voice hollered back. "Come on up. If you're not white, you'll die," a soldier said.

Campbell turned to look at the others. He eyed Rye.

"Truce until this is over," he said.

Rye didn't answer.

"I'll take that as a yes, because if you say anything, the soldiers will hang you pronto, you being a deserter and all."

When they reached the fort, Campbell explained the hardship to the soldiers, the struggles, and the many battles with Sioux warriors.

"Welcome to the fort. I'm Lieutenant Tom Gere," said a young man who looked deathly ill with swollen cheeks and spots covering his face. "I'm sorry you all have to be here under these circumstances. There has been a lot of bloodshed."

"What happened?" Rye asked.

"It's a long story," said another lieutenant named Sheehan, who walked up. "Right now, I don't have time to talk about it. The commanding officer went out yesterday with a troop to the Redwood Ferry. A few of the men made it back." The lieutenant surveyed the group. "I need men to go out on a detail to bring Captain Marsh and the rest of the men home. I can understand if none of you want to do it because it looks like you're all in. However—"

"I'll go," Rye said.

"Who did you say you were?" the lieutenant asked.

"I didn't."

The lieutenant studied him. "As for you others, please feel free to get some rest. There is food for you in the mess hall. We'll need your firepower in the future. I don't know if the Sioux will attack here, but we will be ready." He called for one of the sergeants. "Make sure these people are taken care of."

"Yes, sir," the sergeant responded.

Rye started to walk away, but the lieutenant stopped him.

"What can you tell me about the Indian strength?"

"I am estimating close to a hundred we saw on trails around the river," Rye said. "We ran into patrols throughout our trek to the fort. Five, ten, fifteen as many as two dozen warriors at a time. They're coming from everywhere, burning, raping, looting, and killing."

This time the lieutenant turned and stared at the river. "It was only a matter of time before the valley went up in smoke. There is no stopping it now."

A sergeant approached the two and saluted the lieutenant. "The detail is ready to go," he said.

"Thank you, sergeant," the lieutenant said. "We have one man volunteering to go with you."

"That will be good," the sergeant said, eyeing Rye.

Rye climbed onto the Black.

"Ready, captain," he said.

Rye's eyes darted at the sergeant.

"Don't worry sir, you don't remember me, but you saved my bacon awhile back in Tennessee. Even though a Reb, I never forget a face, especially one who saved my life."

The ten-man detail headed toward the Redwood Ferry.

***

Christina's eyes followed him until the horses were out of sight.

"He will be back," the lieutenant said from behind her.

"I know he will," she said. "He is a brave man. The first time I set my eyes upon him, I knew he would save us. He did. He will again." She walked away.

He watched her go. "I sure hope so, ma'am. I sure hope so."

Chapter 6

After the horse took a few steps, the sergeant started talking. "Yesterday, we only had seventy-five men or so. The lieutenant you first met, the one with the mumps, immediately sent out messengers when he found out Marsh had gone after the Sioux. Now we have a few more men. I don't know if it will be enough."

The men continued down the trail.

"The story goes Marsh knew if he didn't stop the Sioux, the valley would explode. He'd been told he would be outnumbered if he went to the Redwood Ferry. Others who rushed to the fort told him the same thing. He refused to turn back.

"Once the soldiers made it down into the bluffs, they had to leave the wagons and travel by foot single file. Thick grass and heavy growth of hazel and willow brush made the trek difficult, although the growth of hazel and willow offered cover along both sides of the river."

Reb joined in. "We have seen several Indians along the route."

"It sounds like the Indians jumped up out of the trees and bushes and laid siege on them killing at least twelve men, including Quinn, the scout. Marsh found shelter, despite being cut off on three sides. Didn't hear the rest of the story."

Rye listened to all the sergeant had to say.

"The government has made so many promises to the

Natives and has broken every one of them. The post traders have given the Sioux credit and then taken all the annuities due to them when the government checks arrived. Sioux women have been used and abused. Many of the younger warriors are drunk. At one point, a trader told them to eat grass if they were hungry. That would be enough to make me angry."

"I see."

"I've seen some things within the last day you can't imagine. Young babies cut out of women's wombs. One of the traders, Andrew Myrick, died in front of his trading post. The Indians stuck grass in his mouth. Justice."

"They sound desperate," Rye said.

"They are. I'm scared. I don't want to be caught by the Sioux. I've seen what anger can do. There will be no mercy for us."

"And I volunteered for this," Rye said.

The sergeant grinned. "Yeah, you sure did."

Rye stopped his horse. "We've found your captain."

"Oh my God," the sergeant said. In front of them, dead bodies were strewn all over the ground. The ferry had been burned, its operator's body was missing fingers. The soldiers turned their heads. One threw up.

"Sergeant, you'd better have a couple of soldiers keep an eye out for more Indians while we collect the bodies."

The sergeant didn't respond. He stared at the corpses.

"Come on, sergeant, get with it. We have to get these soldiers out of here before more come."

The sergeant hollered. "Smith, Colver, stand guard. The rest of you collect the bodies and place them in the wagons." His hand went to his mouth. A dozen arrows stuck out of many of the corpses. Some body parts lay feet away from their owners. Several of the soldiers ran to the water's edge and puked.

Rye waded into the water. He'd found the captain's floating body before he could identify him. "Sergeant, over here. I think we have the captain."

The sergeant waded his horse out into the water and climbed off. The two dragged the body to shore. The sergeant turned the body over.

"It is Captain Marsh," he said.

"You're right. It looks like an ambush, and they didn't have a chance," Rye said. "The captain doesn't seem to have any wounds. He drowned."

"We need to move," the sergeant said. "Get the men loaded, and let's get out of here."

Rye climbed out of the water to help the sergeant move Captain Marsh into one of the wagons. Rye looked up to see Sioux staring at them.

"What is happening?" the sergeant asked.

"Maybe, they're allowing you to bury your dead."

"Never thought about that."

No chance. The Sioux plunged into the water on foot, firing at the soldiers before they could get organized. Only Rye's sharpshooting and the length of the river crossing allowed the soldiers to get set. As soon as the fight started, the Sioux disappeared, but not before they killed a number of soldiers. The Sioux headed west away from the river. Rye surveyed the remnant crew. The sergeant still had enough men to load the wagon and take the dead back to the fort.

The men struggled to put the bodies in the back of the wagons. It turned out to be a slow process, because the men kept stopping to look for more Indians. Rye stared at the scared group of men heading back toward Fort Ridgely.

Rye sat on his horse for a few moments, scanning the area to make sure they hadn't missed anyone. A soft cry from the right caught Rye's ear. He moved toward the sound, then climbed off the Black, pulled out his pistol, and crept toward the brush. Rye's hand covered his mouth at a sickening sight. The lady had been gutted and the fetus left hanging out of her womb. He buried them.

He crawled back on the Black and rode toward the fort.

A half mile on the trail, Rye ran into four scared men. Eyes distant, gun powder on their faces, and their minds not in the present. An elderly gentleman spoke up.

"When I saw you, I thought you were another damn injun. We've had enough. They killed the men just north of us and might have killed us if not for your burial detail. We decided to head for the fort."

"Are you all there is?"

"No, there are still our women back in the marshes," another said. "I don't know if they're alive or dead."

"You mean you left them?"

"Damn right. I'm not getting my scalp lifted."

"Not even for your loved ones?" Rye asked, his eyes wide.

"Nothing we can do about it."

They moved forward.

Rye rode toward the direction they had suggested, moving at a slow pace to search for other survivors. He couldn't believe that these people would leave their loved ones to be slaughtered by the Sioux, or worse yet, taken hostage.

He rode into a marshy area and stopped the horse. Was that a moan? Rye spoke in a low tone. "It's okay. I'm a white man bringing you home to safety."

The young woman huddled in the marsh was too scared to move. Rye climbed off his horse and knelt down beside her. "It's okay. You're safe now." He took her hand and pulled her up to him. The woman put her arms around Rye. He held her for a few moments until she stopped shaking and sobbing.

"Are you ready to head back to safety?"

Their eyes met for an instant. Rye had seen them once before, but where? He snapped out of it and stood, then reached for her hand once more and pulled her up out of the marsh.

Her ripped clothes fell off her body. She covered her

breasts with her arms. Rye went to his horse, grabbed his blanket, and wrapped it around her.

"It's okay. You're safe now. Is there anyone else with you?"

"All dead," the woman said.

"Come on. Let's get you out of here." Rye lifted her onto the horse.

"My name is Blanche Park."

"Glad to meet you, Blanche Park. I am Rye Tyler."

***

Blanche Park's head snapped up. Her father and others had mentioned this man. The men sent to kill him had failed.

"Thank you, Rye Tyler, for saving my life." She held his hand for a moment, and then let it go.

***

Rye walked the horse further away from the fort. Blanche spoke up, "We're heading away from Fort Ridgely."

Rye glanced up at her. "I know. I ran across some men who said they had left their women along here. I thought I would search around a bit more. I'm sorry, I should have asked if you feel up to it."

"If there are others out there, we should try to find them. I wouldn't want them to fall into the hands of the Sioux."

Rye continued forward with the horse. Every bone ached on his body. But, he was better off than those who went through the Sioux rampage. Just a few more moments, and then they'd turn back if he didn't find any signs of the women.

***

Blanche Park crawled off the horse and walked next to him. Her eyes followed the man she'd heard of, although she'd never met him. Libbie always talked about him. Rye wouldn't know Blanche because she arrived after he left; a swap of sorts. Rye stood about six-foot-two, she estimated based on her five-nine-inch frame. She stood taller than most of the women she knew in the valley. Only her sister stood as tall. And this man. Rye. She pulled the blanket over her.

"Are you warm enough?"

"What?" she said.

Rye stopped. "Here, let me grab a shirt out of my pack, so you have something to cover your body."

He reached into his bag and pulled out a shirt, then turned around so she could slip it on.

Blanche tapped him on the shoulder. "You can turn around now." The shirt covered the upper part of her body and draped halfway down her legs.

"Does that feel better?"

"Yes, it does. Thank you."

"You're welcome."

The two walked toward the north. Fires burned to the west, masking the sunset. Neither said a word. Blanche continued to measure him up. A handsome man with gorgeous blue eyes. His brown, curly hair went down to his shoulders. She surmised the bandanna tied around his head kept the hair out of his eyes. Even though a soldier, he didn't act the part.

Enough, she said to herself. You have to get to safety. There is no place for a man in your life; especially this man.

Chapter 7

The sun had set by the time the sergeant and the detail made it back to the fort. The Sioux had made no effort to follow them. Lieutenant Gere walked over to the sergeant. The sergeant saluted, and the lieutenant returned the salute.

"Captain Marsh is among the dead," the sergeant said.

"I know. The troops who returned told me."

"Without bringing back their dead?" the sergeant spat out.

The lieutenant didn't say anything, but his frown said it all. "Get them properly buried, sergeant. You did a good job. Where is Tyler?"

"He stayed out there to keep an eye on the Sioux. Should be in anytime." The sergeant explained what had happened with the Indians on the bluff.

"You couldn't do anything else. I'm just glad you brought back who you could alive," Lieutenant Gere said.

***

For Rye, it turned out to be slow going. The dusk settled upon them quickly, and they still had many miles to travel before arriving at the fort. Ready to give up the search and take Blanche Park back to the fort, he stumbled across three battered ladies.

The three just sat and stared at the bush in front of them, mumbling. Neither Rye nor Blanche could understand their words.

"We are here to help you," Blanche said. Still no word.

Just stares. Rye handed the reins of the horse to Blanche. He knelt down and peered into the eyes of one of the women, then slapped her across the face. She broke into hysterics. Rye pulled her close to him and patted her back to calm her down. Softly, he said, "We have come to bring you home."

She stared up at him. "I'm Sarah. Please don't let the Indians take me."

Rye glanced at Blanche. He looked back at the woman. "They won't harm you while I'm with you."

Sarah clung to his chest. He nodded for Blanche to come over and help. She did just that and Rye handed Sarah over to her. He returned to the other two women. The same. Mumbling and making no sense to him.

Rye helped the second lady up off the ground. Blood splayed around her. She had tried to stab herself. Rye cleaned up the blood on her leg the best he could, then went to his horse and brought a wrap to staunch the bleeding. That done, Rye walked her over to the horse and helped her up onto the saddle. "Please hold onto the saddle horn."

She did as he asked.

Rye went back for the third lady. This woman kept casting furtive glances around her. She stared up at Rye. Dead eyes. Rye reached down and picked her up into his arms and carried her over to the horse. The woman had been so weak she huddled into his shoulder and started crying.

***

Blanche studied the man holding the woman tight. A deadly man with a kind heart. It couldn't be possible.

Once he calmed the three women down a bit, Rye handed Blanche the reins. "Please take them and walk the ladies. I will help Sarah."

"I can do that."

"I have no doubt, Blanche Park. You are a strong woman." He trudged along with Sarah. Blanche followed the man until she caught up and walked next to him.

They walked for about an hour in silence and progressed

only about a mile. As the sky darkened, it became even more of a struggle. The moon high in the sky and the continued silhouette of the fires throughout the valley helped pave the way.

One of the ladies on the horses started screaming.

Blanche tried to quiet her down. "Ma'am, it will be okay. We'll make it."

"I know we will. He has come." The woman stared at Rye who had come up beside them. "I prayed for an angel. He showed up. I just didn't think it would be a man with such long hair. And a bandana wrapped around the forehead to boot."

Blanche smiled.

They reached the ferry. Blanche helped the ladies down and found them a place to sit and rest. One lady sat down next to her. "Your man?"

"Oh gosh, no," Blanche responded.

The woman watched Rye help Sarah and then turn back to Blanche. "I believe that someday you'll try to destroy him. It won't work because you'll fall in love with him."

Blanche didn't know how to respond. In a flash the Sioux swooped down around and encircled them. The women screamed.

***

Rye pulled out his pistol. It couldn't kill them all.

"It would do no good, white man. We could have killed you earlier," a voice said in English.

The sun had set, and the faces were hard to distinguish, but this was the band of Sioux Rye had seen across the river.

The chief peered at Reb. "You are a brave warrior." Rye didn't say anything.

An argument ensued among the chief and several of the Sioux. The chief calmly turned back to Rye and he stared at the older women. "The young warriors want the young woman. They want to butcher you because you are a white man."

Rye didn't say anything for a moment. He studied Blanche. "Please go to the women and protect them."

***

At that moment, Blanche realized this man would be hard to destroy. But she knew that someday she would have to bury him. "Stop thinking like that," she said to herself.

"You will not take these women as captives," Rye said to the Indian. "I probably will die tonight. But if I do, you and several of your young warriors will die also. I have nothing to lose. Can you say the same?"

The two stared at each other. One warrior ran at him. Rye shot him point-blank between the eyes. Another followed and received the same fate. Each time Rye pointed his pistol back at the chief. "I don't want to kill you. All I want is to take these women to safety."

The chief raised his voice, and the warriors stopped in their tracks. He motioned to some warriors who brought up four horses. "Take the horses and these people to the soldier's house." He started to turn and then stopped. His eyes narrowed at Rye. "We will not kill you … for now. Make no mistake. Next time we meet, it won't end this way." With a glance at Blanche, he rode away.

"You would have killed them all if you had to?" Blanche asked Rye quietly.

"Yes, I would have."

She helped the ladies onto the horses. Rye didn't say anything but stared at the chief's wake. That look the chief gave Blanche. What did it mean?

"We had better move. We're not too far away from the fort," Blanche said.

Rye packed the ladies upon the horses and headed toward the fort. The health of the women and the darkness made it even tougher than before. After midnight, the small group arrived.

***

The sergeant ran toward them.

"I begged the lieutenant to let me go out after you. He wouldn't let me. But you sure did bring in a passel of people, and I mean angry women. A couple of them actually slugged their husbands. I had to chuckle. They are that mad," the sergeant said.

"I'm just glad they made it in," Rye said and turned to walk away.

"Where are you heading?"

"I'm finding a place to sleep...at least for a week."

The sergeant laughed. Rye found a pile of loose straw and dropped directly into it. It wasn't a moment before he fell asleep.

***

"I see you're still alive, Blanche."

She swung around to see Libbie staring at her.

"And you brought him back with you."

"I don't even know who he is."

Libbie eyed her. "You know who he is. That's where our mother and father sent you."

"He just showed up. I went for a ride with a man."

"Where is he?"

"Butchered like the others were out there. Too bad you weren't one of them."

"What are you and the family up to?"

"It doesn't concern you, Libbie. You just play your part."

Libbie didn't say anything. Blanche smiled at her.

"Well, sister, don't get too attached to him. He won't live much longer." With that Libbie walked away. A tinge of anger stirred in her bones. All her life Libbie had meant nothing to anyone. She looked back at Rye Tyler. Different than anyone she had ever met, he had always meant something to her. Just maybe, she would mean something to him. Why had her sister gone out into the river area?

Blanche's father walked over and put his arm around her. "What were you thinking going out there?"

"I didn't know, father."

"At least you're safe. Now you need to stay with the young Tyler."

"Why not just kill him?"

"It is not that easy. Just keep your eye on him and stay with him. I'm counting on you to move him out west. Sleep with him. Do whatever you need to do."

"Wouldn't it be easier to use Libbie?"

Her father peered at Blanche. "Whatever you do, don't let Libbie influence him in any way. He may just take her away. Then we'll never find him. We're not done with him yet."

"I understand, father."

Chapter 8

The next morning, Rye felt a tug at his shirt. He opened his eyes. Isabelle stared at him with a smile. He smiled back. Rye sat up, and the girl jumped into his arms. "What are you up to?"

"Nothing. I came to check on you."

Lieutenant Sheehan assigned everyone to different locations around the fort. Rye and the sergeant helped others cover the ravines to the east. Sheehan expected that to be the toughest area to defend.

By lunchtime, one soldier noticed movement to the west. A few shots were fired. The main body of the Sioux didn't move up through the ravines until later. Suddenly a blood-curdling scream sounded as Sioux warriors emerged from the ravines. Sheehan had set up a battle line on the parade ground. As the casualties grew larger, the men had to fall back.

The artillery started hammering the perimeter. That and the sharpshooting of Rye and the sergeant, standing side-by-side, scattered the Sioux back into the ravine.

"That's fancy shooting for a northerner," Rye said, smiling.

"You're not too bad yourself for a rebel," the sergeant countered.

The Sioux continued to fire from a distance the rest of the day. Rye helped move the supplies that sat on the exposed prairie to a spot within the fort perimeter. Others kept their eyes peeled for Sioux. No one knew how many had gone down in the battle. The Sioux dragged off their dead quickly, making it impossible to get an accurate death count.

After he helped move the supplies, Rye dropped to the ground, beat. He rubbed his neck to loosen up the joints. The sergeant peered at him, shook his head, and walked away. Rye contemplated his next move. With no ties to this country, he could crawl onto the Black and head west. But, he still had to avenge the death of the young soldiers in Murfreesboro.

"I see you're deep in thought," a voice spoke up.

Rye glanced up, saw the boots, then shapely, bronzed legs, then the skirt and blouse that showed her firm breasts, and then her glowing face with sparkling blue eyes and a beautiful smile. The woman called Libbie with a bandanna tied around her head stood above him. She bent down on one knee and handed Rye a plate of food.

"Here, you probably need this."

"Thanks," he said to her. He savored the beans and potatoes. "I see you clean up fairly decently."

She didn't say anything but kneeled behind him. "Let me rub your shoulders."

***

Libbie used her fingers to relax the tense muscle in his shoulders. She wanted so much to tell him she missed him and wanted him to take her away. Instead she said, "I never got to say thank you for saving my sister's life."

Rye turned and looked at Libbie. "Blanche Park is your sister?"

"She went by Park, I see. That is her middle name."

"Nothing to thank me for. I happened to be there at the right time."

Libbie smiled. "You didn't have to be."

"I couldn't sit around and do nothing."

"Who are you? Why are you here?"

"Why would you ask that?"

"Because most of the men around here wouldn't have gone out of their way to do something like that. And I might admit—" she added smiling, "it's kind of crazy, if you ask me."

"I wouldn't disagree with you on that. Where is your family?"

"They're all dead," she said.

He changed the subject. "The blouse and skirt look good on you. You are a beautiful woman."

She smiled. "Thank you. I bet you don't say that to too many women."

Rye blushed. "You're the first one I've ever said it to."

Libbie had a slight smile he couldn't see. For several moments both sat silently as Libbie continued to stretch out the tightness in Rye's shoulders. She also worked on his back and finally she felt the tension ease up. "There, I hope that will help you relax."

He smiled at her. "It feels wonderful. This is probably the most relaxed I've felt in some time. Are you sure you wouldn't want to stay here and continue to do this?"

She smiled back at him. "It is tempting, but I'm sure you would rather get some sleep." Libbie then got up and started to walk away but turned before she'd gone too far. "Will I see you again?"

He smiled. "If your fingers are that relaxing, yes." Then his expression changed. "But I have unfinished business to settle."

"You should have left my sister. She will be your demise." The two gazed at each other. She knew he wanted to take her away. "Don't. All I'll do is get you killed. I won't do that to you."

Libbie walked away, her mind racing. She cared about this man deeply. She couldn't be part of his destruction. Rye Tyler, the man she'd longed for these past eleven years, had returned, and Libbie couldn't do a thing about it.

***

The second person who said Blanche Park would be his demise. Rye lay back down and fell asleep immediately. Against his better judgment, he thought it wise to keep Blanche Davis near him. Enemies and all. Although he'd rather leave and take Libbie with him.

Things had changed. One man he looked for turned into three children. He couldn't leave them unprotected. Rye didn't know if Libbie even cared about him anymore. It had been a long time. He would bide his time.

The next day the rains hit, and everyone did what they could to stay dry.

Rye headed toward the stable to saddle the Black. He had to get out of there and fast. He'd ride west and he would find Butler Lily.

"You can't leave, mister," Campbell said.

Rye ignored him and saddled his horse. A pistol cocked behind his right ear. He whipped around. Another soldier had walked up beside Campbell.

"What is this?"

"You aren't going anywhere."

"Just like Murfreesboro, I see. Campbell, you need to hide behind someone else and can't fight your own battles."

"He's here because I told the lieutenant exactly who you were. Now that the fighting is over, I'll have the pleasure of bringing you to justice and watching you hang. I'm under orders to put you in the guardhouse until you can be transported out of here."

Rye tried to reach his gun.

"Don't think about it, Tyler," Campbell said. "I would rather just as soon plug you now than let you escape out of here again. There's no way out of swinging from a rope."

Two of the soldiers walked over to Rye.

"Sorry sir," one said. "Our orders."

Quickly, Rye swung around, grabbed the pistol, and pointed it at Campbell. His eyes widened, as did those of the soldiers who watched the altercation. "We can end it here, Campbell, or we can join forces and fight the Sioux. Or I could just kill you right now and fight the Sioux myself. It makes no difference to me."

Campbell didn't move. Libbie and Blanche looked on and appeared amazed at how Rye scared the man. Campbell pivoted and stalked away. Rye flipped the pistol and gave it back to the corporal. "Sorry, corporal. I just don't like that guy."

Rye collapsed in his little corner of his world in a pile of straw. This time he didn't fall right to sleep. He thought about Libbie, the same girl he knew at ten years old. She'd turned into a beautiful woman. Her smile and glowing blue eyes made her that much more attractive. Picturing the golden-brown hair that cascaded over her shoulders, framing her face like a picture, he fell asleep. Her sister, Blanche looked exactly the same. They could be twins.

The next morning Isabelle came with something to eat.

"Well thank you, ma'am," he said.

She smiled at him.

"For a ten-year-old, you sure are responsible."

She sat with him as he ate. "When you leave, will you take me with you?"

"I can't, little one."

"Oh, I see."

She rose but stopped. "One day, sir, I will be with you. Then, I'll feel safe for the first time in my life."

Rye watched her walk away not knowing what to think. He lay back down to rest some more but woke up with a start when shots fired. People screamed.

Isabelle ran over to him, seized his hand, and held it tight. "The Indians are back."

Rye scrambled out of the straw, lifted Isabelle into his arms, and ran to a spot where the Sioux had broken through the day before. This time he couldn't see anything.

"Where are they?" the sergeant asked.

Rye pointed over to an area where he saw movement. "They've camouflaged their headbands with prairie grass and flowers."

"Those devious fiends," the sergeant said.

Rye motioned for Isabelle to get down. She hid behind the barrier. Rye aimed his rifle and knocked one of the Sioux down. He scrambled back into the ravine.

Rye whirled around at the sound of an assault in the southwest—hand-to-hand combat with the warriors.

Other Indians had made it to the stables and released livestock.

The duo joined others trying to keep the livestock in the pens. It turned out to be a losing effort. The Sioux also set fires. Soldiers worked to repel the charge. The livestock broke out and ran through the fort grounds. Those scurrying out to fight the Sioux dodged animals. Some warriors used the animals as shields to get up close.

Two Indians charged Rye, but he quickly killed them with his pistol. Isabelle ran over to him. He picked her up and carried her behind one of the wagons. Libbie joined them.

"Watch over Isabelle," he said.

They turned when shells went off again killing Sioux and scattering them back into the prairie. The three hid behind a turned-over wagon that had been burned earlier. Rye sensed something behind him. He flipped his pistol and drilled an Indian who'd snuck through toward the wagon.

Another jumped on him from behind. Rye slapped the knife away from him as he tried to bury it into Rye's chest. Out of the corner of his eye, he saw Libbie fighting off a warrior. Another had picked up Isabelle and was running toward the ravine. Rye shot him in the back of the head. The bullet whistled inches from Isabelle's head.

When the Indian fell, he sprinted to Isabelle to pick her up. Too late. Another warrior grabbed the young girl and headed down the ravine. Libbie struggled with the Sioux.

Rye grabbed the warrior's arm, swung him around, and buried the knife in his chest.

He ran to the top of the ravine, aimed the rifle, and nailed the Sioux. He dropped Isabelle. Rye ran down to get the young girl. She jumped into his arms and held him tight. Rye carried her up to the others.

At the top of the ravine, Christina ran to grab her sister. "Thank you, Rye," she said.

He smiled at her and then turned when his horse trotted toward him. He talked quietly to him, Rye then tightened the strap on his horse.

"Are you leaving?" Libbie asked him.

He swung up on the Black. "I'm looking for a man." Rye tipped his hat and rode off toward the ravine.

***

Libbie and Christina jumped at shots fired. They watched as the horse bolted toward the ravine and out into the river.

"What happened?" Blanche asked.

The sergeant and several others ran to the ravine, including the lieutenant and Price Davis. Campbell told the lieutenant that he had fired the shot to keep him from escaping.

Sheehan gazed out toward the horizon. "That Confederate's fate is now up to God and the Sioux."

They walked away. Libbie stared to the west.

"Please do something?" Christina asked her.

Libbie looked at Christina. Then she saddled a horse and chased after Rye.

***

Rye saw the blood on the saddle before he felt the pain. He climbed off the mustang and checked for the wound. Touching his right side under his shirt, he pulled out a handful of blood.

Pressing the wound with his right hand, Rye used his left one to open his saddlebag to find something to stop the bleeding. Pain shot through his right abdomen, and he fell to the ground. The mustang hovered over his body.

The last thing Rye remembered was a woman's quiet voice.

Chapter 9

Rye woke up startled. Everything looked fuzzy. He struggled to move, but the dizziness caused him to fall back down on the ground. He was inside a shelter of some sort.

A soft voice told him to relax. He looked toward the voice, thought he saw a woman staring at him, and fell again. When Rye woke up a second time, a fire glowed in the dark.

He didn't try to get up this time. "Where am I?"

"You are safe for now," the voice whispered to him. "Please, you need to get your rest. We will talk after, when you get the rest you need."

Rye fell asleep a third time.

***

Blanche glanced at Libbie. "I'll take over from here. Don't ever get in the middle of Rye and me again."

Libbie stared at her sister. "Don't you hurt him."

"Or what?" Blanche laughed at her. "Go away now before I send Otaktay after you. You know how he feels about you."

A frightened Libbie climbed on her horse and rode back to Fort Ridgely.

Blanche stirred the fire to keep Rye warm. She peered at the man lying on the ground. Her older sister had dug two bullets out of him. Neither life-threatening, but he had lost blood.

Libbie brought him to a safe location for the time being.

The Sioux would find them sooner or later. She hoped it would be later in order for Rye to gain back some strength. Either way a grim situation loomed ahead for him. He couldn't die yet. Blanche needed to keep him alive. She must get him out west.

Blanche dozed off near Rye but jumped when he stirred. "Take it easy. You've lost a lot of blood," she said.

"What are you doing here?"

"I'm trying to save your life."

"Thank you." He struggled to sit up but failed. Blanche helped him up.

He fell back down on the ground and within moments closed his eyes. Rye drifted into a deep sleep, Blanche covered him up with a blanket and fell asleep near him.

A slight drizzle woke both of them up. Rye stared at Blanche.

"What?" she asked.

"You are not the person I saw yesterday."

Blanche moved away from him. "We have to get you out of here. I've bought us some time, but the Sioux will find this location. Can you move?

"Yes, I think so." He struggled to get up. She helped him by putting his arms over her shoulders. The two made it to the clearing. The mustang knelt down on his front legs to make it easier for Rye, and Blanche helped him onto the Black. She climbed upon another horse.

"This way," she pointed.

He followed her. After about a half hour of riding through a series of culverts and trees, they came to an opening along a river. "Where are we?" Rye asked.

"We are at the Redwood River. East leads us back to the fort. West leads us into Dakota Territory. It is your choice."

"Why are you doing this?" Rye asked.

"You saved my life. Now, I return the favor."

"What about you?"

She didn't respond. They continued to ride west.

"How did you escape from the fort?" Rye asked after an hour of silence.

"With all the commotion, I grabbed a horse and followed you. You'd been shot by one of the post guards. When I found you, the Sioux had you surrounded."

She continued. "Your horse wouldn't allow the Indians to take you. The Black continued to circle you. The Sioux looked astonished and stayed away. Then the weirdest thing happened. The Black bolted, dragging you with your foot somehow hooked in the stirrup. The Sioux looked stunned but didn't chase you. I went around to the south and found you. Your foot had fallen out of the stirrup not far from here. I dragged you to a place I felt would be safe. At least until you got some strength back."

"Thank you," Rye said.

"You are welcome."

Rye peered back up the trail. Thought he'd heard movement. The mustang also seemed restless.

"What is it, Rye?"

"There's something out there." Rye drew his pistol and rode across the river. Once across, Blanche and he headed into a grove of trees, and Rye fell off his horse. Blanche jumped off and scrambled to help him. Rye struggled to sit up, Blanche held the horse while Rye climbed back on and checked their back trail. A few moments later, the Sioux rode out of the other side of the river. They stopped and scanned the area.

"Little Crow and his men," Blanche whispered.

Rye turned to her. He'd heard of him.

Five other warriors followed behind Little Crow in a single file. He halted and studied the spot Blanche and Rye had crossed over the river. He glanced toward the grove of trees. The Sioux chief knew where they were.

Blanche climbed onto her horse. This time Rye took the lead. He grabbed the mustang, motioned Blanche to follow him through the grove, and touched his lips with one finger.

Rye didn't know which direction to take, but they had to move quickly. Once the Sioux crossed the river, it would be tough going for the duo. They rode approximately a mile before emerging from a grove of trees on the east side of the river. Rye scanned both sides, then climbed on his horse. Blanche did the same.

The water roiled, but Rye chanced it and started toward the west side of the river. He didn't know where the Sioux were. Nor did he know if Little Crow sent warriors up the river on the same side.

The answer came quickly. A band of warriors rode out of the grove firing at the two. They struggled to reach the other bank of the turbulent river while under Sioux fire. Once out of the water, the two spurred the mustang toward the open plains. They needed space between them and the Sioux.

"Rye, to the left," Blanche hollered.

Six warriors raced toward them. Rye pointed toward the west. The two crossed the field. The Sioux howled as the chase began. Suddenly to the right, another group came out of a draw toward them.

Rye spurred the horse back toward the west. The Sioux tried to pin the two from three different sides. The warriors herded the duo into the only open direction, a trap, but they had no other choice.

"Ahead is a gully," Blanche said.

The mustang came to the top of the gully, and Rye spurred the Black into the gully with Blanche right behind him. The horses raced through it, putting some distance between the Sioux. A half a mile down the gully, they came to a dead end. The horses struggled up the dirt wall but finally pulled through and raced once more into the open plains.

Another mile of running the horses had given Rye and Blanche some breathing room. The pace had taken its toll on the two horses. They had to find somewhere to hole up and rest, or their luck would finally run out.

Rye fell off the horse onto the ground. Blanche quickly climbed down off hers. The wound had opened, and blood seeped out of Rye's chest. She tore off a piece from her skirt and wrapped it as best she could.

Blanche shook him. "Please wake up. We have to go somewhere safe."

His eyes opened quickly. She helped him up, and the two walked toward the west, leading the horses. Neither had any idea where the route would take them. Rye staggered like a disoriented drunk. But he wasn't drunk, and ideas swam around in his head.

"What is it, Rye?"

Rye turned around. "What is happening?"

"I can't tell you. But they will kill you."

"Who will kill me?"

She hesitated and then answered, "The men you've been chasing."

Chapter 10

A third Fort Ridgely attack never materialized.

"What happened?" Campbell asked.

"I don't know," Price Davis said. "It's like the Sioux just disappeared. Maybe it is finally over."

More people straggled in from the countryside. All talked about being relieved that the rampage was over. With eyes brimming with tears, many described their harrowing experience, tales of bloodshed and atrocities, stories of burning homes, the murder of children, even infants still in the womb. Then it had stopped, just like the siege on Fort Ridgely.

"One morning there were warriors screaming. The next moment silence," one man told Lieutenant Sheehan.

Everyone pitched in to help those in need by providing food and clothes. Some had not slept for days. Others had hidden in the brush for days afraid to breathe. One family had traveled thirty miles from the south to the fort because they didn't know where to go for safety.

Several told the same story about a young white man who defied the Sioux, now the target of one of the largest Sioux manhunts since the days of the Sioux and Chippewa wars.

"This man won't survive out there," said a grizzled old man who joined the conversation. "In fact, I wouldn't be surprised if they don't skin him alive piece by piece."

"How do you know any of this?" Libbie asked.

"I've heard the same story numerous times. I tend to believe it to be true."

More people gathered around.

"The Sioux are divided right now. There are some who want to attack New Ulm, others the fort. Still others want this young man because they believe his spirit is powerful. It will only be a matter of time before they catch him. The Sioux know every inch of this land. I hate to see anybody die like he will, but I'm grateful to him for giving me a chance to live. I recommend you use this information to take these people to safety."

The old man shuffled away from the fort toward the New Ulm road.

Lieutenant Sheehan joined the group. "We're taking you all to New Ulm. Please be ready to go as soon as possible."

Within hours the Fort Ridgely evacuation started.

A frustrated Libbie Davis looked to the west. Rye was the man they had been talking about—a pawn who would not only help her family become rich, but also help the South win the war. He'd escaped for the time being; she was thankful for that. Just then Libbie ran into Mina.

"What do you want?"

"Blanche escaped with him."

"How did that happen?"

"They didn't find either of them. They're still looking."

"Do you think she said anything?"

"I'm not sure, but things are going as planned. Blanche is doing her job."

"Butler Lily should be here soon and then it will begin," Libbie said. When Mina turned, Libbie cast a quick glance to the west.

***

Rye and Blanche struggled to find shelter from the Sioux in a wide open area. After three miles of walking, the two climbed back on their horses and rode for another half hour.

"Over there, Rye," Blanche whispered for a second time.

68

Rye saw a gully in the bluffs almost as soon as the words came out of her mouth. He raced toward them. The bluffs kept them hidden as they traveled to the gully. After a half mile, they took a break. Rye's body ached and Blanche looked plain tired. She looked ragged and her eyes were bloodshot. He marveled at this young woman who had defied death to save his life. "We should be fine for at least a little while," Rye said. "We both need the rest. You are a real trooper, Blanche."

She didn't answer the comment but said, "I agree. We need to rest."

"It will take the Sioux some time before they figure out we're here. By then, hopefully we'll be in Dakota Territory."

"We are in the Dakota Territory."

"We need to talk," he said. "What is this all about? Why are you helping me?"

"I said earlier I couldn't let you die for helping me when you did," Blanche peered up at Rye.

"But, now you are an outcast among your people."

"No different than you, Rye. They would have skinned you alive. You saved my life."

They started walking once more.

Rye and Blanche continued another hour before coming out of the gully. Rye did not immediately step out. Sweat poured down him, not only because of the struggle, but also because of not knowing what could be ahead. His eyes darted to the left and the right before finally figuring it was safe.

"Do you have any clue where we are?"

"I don't know."

Blanche handed Rye some buffalo jerky. He took a piece and chewed slowly.

"Don't eat too much because we still have a ways to walk before we get to safety," she said. "We need to keep moving. Like you said we have to find somewhere safe."

Rye didn't say anything but stared to the west. He could

look forever and not see the end.

It took at least another hour before the duo happened upon a burned-out shelter. Rye pulled out his pistol and inched toward it. There wasn't much left, but the building still had a roof attached, which would keep them out of the elements. He slowly pushed the door open. Blanche touched his left hip and stayed close to him, but he pushed her back. Once inside, he found two charred bodies. The charring made them unrecognizable. Rye turned away, covering his face.

"Don't come in, Blanche. They're dead."

Rye walked toward a lean-to. He looked inside and saw nothing.

"We can rest up here," he said. "We'll get some sleep and then continue on in the morning. I have to give those settlers some kind of burial." He looked around for a shovel or some kind of tool to dig a grave. Rye couldn't find one, so he started digging with his hands. Despite slow going, he plugged away.

Meanwhile, Blanche kept an eye out around the area.

Rye built up a sweat from the heat of the sun, but he finally felt he had the hole deep enough to place the bodies. He went back to the house, wrapped them in the remains of a blanket, and placed them into the grave. It took him another twenty minutes to fill in the grave. After, he said a prayer over the couple.

Back at the shelter, Rye moved the saddle to an area on the dirt floor near Blanche. "Here you go. You get some rest and I'll keep an eye out."

"What about you?"

"Get some sleep and I'll wake you up in a couple of hours."

"Don't forget," she said. Blanche closed her eyes and fell asleep.

Rye sat on the dirt floor pointing his rifle toward the east. His thoughts quickly went to Libbie Davis. She might know more about Butler Lily. Maybe it would be best for him to go back and find out. But he'd be borrowing more trouble. They'd hang him on sight at this point. Rye would bide his time.

***

A tall, muscular man followed by four horsemen rode into Fort Ridgely. Everyone turned to them. Libbie frowned at the sight.

"Butler," she said.

"Libbie, it is good to see you once more."

Price Davis walked up to him. "Well, Butler, why didn't you take care of your business? Twice you had the opportunity and you failed."

"It's not over yet," he said. "It may be a good thing that we kept him alive."

"I thought that also. Blanche is taking him west."

"I just came from that direction, and there is more money for us if you wish."

Price smiled. "I do."

Butler Lily smiled back at him. "Different areas of the West are having silver and gold strikes. We can step right in and literally make a killing on all of it."

"And why would you suggest I leave this area of the country?"

"Look around you, Price. The country is up in smoke. The Indians are pissed. And they will be coming for you. Besides, it will put more into the country's coffers. And most importantly, Blanche will be bringing Rye Tyler to us to help us conquer the West."

Price Davis looked at him with a furrowed brow.

"Price, he knows where the gold bullion is."

This brought a smile to Davis's face.

"Maybe it is best to get out of here before it becomes too late. What do you think, dear?" he asked, turning to his wife.

"Butler is right. It's probably better to get away from here."

"What about Tyler?" Lily asked.

"I agree with Butler. We'll run into him again. Blanche has never let us down."

"Well then, let's gather everything up and head west. No time to lose. How many men do we have left?"

"At least two dozen willing to continue the quest."

Butler Lily said, "That should be plenty."

After he said that, he saw Libbie staring at him with narrowed eyes. "What?"

"Nothing. I wondered how you would feel knowing Rye will never tell you where the gold bullion is."

"Oh yes he will, dear. Rye will do anything to protect you."

Libbie glared at him, turned, and started to walk away. She stopped. "That is not the same Rye Tyler I knew when we were younger. He is deadly. He'd just as soon kill me, especially when he finds out what I've done."

He gazed at her, thinking he'd like to take her for his own someday.

Chapter 11

Rye had stepped outside of the lean-to and looked back toward the east. Even as far away as they had traveled, smoke filled the air. Blanche started to stir. She stretched and pushed herself off the floor.

"How long did I sleep?"

"All night long."

"Why didn't you wake me up?"

"I got some sleep too. I wasn't tired, so I just let you sleep. Besides, it looked like you needed it."

***

Blanche gathered their things and packed them in the saddlebag. Rye stepped back outside. When Blanche came out, he was staring toward the east. She touched his arm. He turned to look at her. "Rye, we can go back there if you wish, but we struggled to get this far. It doesn't make any sense to go back."

He started walking toward the west. She grabbed his arm to stop him. He swung around.

"I know that you have vengeance on your mind, Riley Tyler. I can accept that, and I will help you anyway I can. But you have to understand something."

He hesitated for a moment.

Blanche forced him to look into her eyes. Standing on her tiptoes, she met his eyes. "I have a lot to tell you, but I don't know where to start."

"You're part of all that is happening."

73

"Yes. I am. But that all changed when you saved me in the slough."

Rye didn't say anything at first. Finally, he spoke. "I've been a loner all of my life. My family shipped me away at a young age. Even during the war, I didn't feel comfortable around those who fought by my side." He hesitated once more. "I don't trust you, Blanche Park. You and the others want me to do something. I'll play along for Libbie's sake and because I'm hunting down three men. You know who they are." He batted Blanche's arm away and stormed off.

Blanche shook her head and followed. *Damn Libbie.* She loved this man and would ruin everything. Blanche could see it in the way Libbie looked at him. And she could tell Rye cared a lot about Libbie. Blanche would have to do something to sway Rye toward her and away from her sister. She understood why.

***

Rye and Blanche finally stopped after having traveled at least three hours on foot. Rye gazed to the west and still could see for miles. He turned at the screech. A warrior raced toward them. Rye shoved Blanche to the ground as an arrow whizzed by her.

Rye fired a quick shot from the hip, and the Indian screamed and fell to the ground. He looked around and saw a steep bluff. It would provide some cover from the Indians who'd homed in on this site. He grabbed Blanche's hand.

The two scrambled up the bank and slid behind the bluffs for protection. At least six Sioux had seen them. Two Sioux warriors rode up on their horses. Rye quickly fired at one, then with two shots, he killed the other. The rest scattered.

"It looks like they're running toward the west," Rye said. "There'll be more running away from Minnesota."

Both sat quiet for a moment. Rye looked up at the sun that was setting in the distance. "This is as good a place to rest as any," Rye said. He lowered himself behind a place he thought would provide some protection from the Sioux and shelter from the elements. Blanche sat down next to him. He fell asleep and didn't wake up until the next morning. Blanche was still sleeping. He crept to the clearing and made a small fire, went to his horse, and pulled out a coffeepot and coffee. A few moments later Blanche woke up to the smell of coffee.

"Where are we?" she asked, taking a cup from him.

"I don't know."

She touched him softly. "Why don't you let the past go and find that solitude you've been yearning for?"

Rye peered up at Blanche. "It's not that simple."

"It can be if you wish."

"You're a hopeful person, Blanche Park."

"Rye Tyler, ever since you came to Minnesota, the deck has been stacked against you. Butler Lily is after you. Our families want to kill you. The Sioux want your scalp. And if that isn't enough, there's a man named Marcus Duncan coming after you."

His eyes looked dark. It scared her, especially after what she'd seen him do.

Rye didn't say anything. He just enjoyed this momentary peace and his coffee.

"What does the name Marcus Duncan mean to you?"

"Nothing."

***

She didn't push it. That name meant something to him. And she knew exactly what. Blanche circled the rim of her coffee cup with her finger. "At ten I had a crush on you. One moment I enjoyed playing with you. The next day you left. What happened to you?"

Rye didn't react, just stared at the sky like he always did. She had to do something before she lost him.

"I don't remember you at all. I don't remember your family, my family, nothing about Minnesota. Or maybe I chose to blank it out," he finally said.

Blanche waited for him to continue. When he didn't, she filled in the silence. "Two years ago, everything started. My family shipped me East to college. I never understood why until I returned. Or I should say my father called me back to marry a man named Ben Raven."

Rye's eyes lit up. "You what?"

"You know the man?"

"You married that man? I knew him."

"Ben knew you also. He sent Butler Lily to Tennessee to kill you. As you're breathing, it never materialized." She smiled and went on. "You kind of screwed that up by surviving."

Rye's lips curved into a half smile.

"Our families made a mint off of the Indians. Butler and my father made sure your name circulated as the person behind the Sioux issues. Marcus Duncan's orders. I've only met the man two or three times, but they seem to be afraid of him."

"How are you involved?"

"I kept the money coming in until the Sioux captured me, or I should say, Marcus turned me in to save himself. You saved me. Once I heard the name Rye Tyler, it spooked me. Everyone said you're an evil killer. But you risked your life saving those people. I don't know why."

Rye stared at Blanche. "There are a couple of things you need to know. I am a killer. I trained others to be the same."

Her eyes widened. "I don't see that in you. I see a man who loves life and got a raw deal."

"You're an intelligent woman, and you see the best in people."

"And the second thing?"

Rye stood. "I don't trust people. There is only one person I will ever trust. Let's move."

At that moment a Sioux warrior jumped on Blanche. They grappled with each other. He started to rip her blouse, when Rye's arm snaked around his neck. She cringed at the crack of bone. Rye threw the Indian off of her.

Another warrior joined the fight as Rye and the previous Indian tussled. Blanche pulled Rye's pistol out of his holster and fired a shot at the Indian. It missed the target.

Rye broke away from the warrior, took the pistol from Blanche, and shot the warrior who had come from the other side of the bluff. Rye pushed Blanche behind him and stopped the warrior's knife with his arm. He spun him around and snapped his neck with a quick jerk. "Are you okay, Blanche?"

She ran over to him and buried her head in his arms. "Thank you. Again, you saved my life. You're bleeding," Blanche said. "Here, let me look at it." She quickly took off his shirt. A wound had opened on his chest. "Do you have a death wish? Where did you get all those scars?"

Rye didn't say anything.

"I'm sorry," Blanche said. "I didn't mean that. I'm rattled."

"I understand," Rye said. "I don't think they'll be back. We should move on." Rye climbed up onto the Black and stared down at the woman. "You're wrong about one thing."

Blanche waited.

"I'm no different than the Natives out here. I'm a butcher."

Blanche glanced his way. "One thing you also need to know, I never married Raven."

Rye turned and rode the horse toward the west. Blanche climbed on her horse. For the remainder of the day, the two traveled in silence until they came to a lake. Rye stopped the horse. She followed his lead.

"We should be okay here for the night," he said. Blanche didn't say anything. She gathered wood to start a fire. Rye loosened the cinch on the Black's saddle. He didn't take it off, nor did he tie the horse. The Black wouldn't leave him.

Blanche cooked food. Both ate without speaking. Too much to think about. When it was dark, Blanche fell asleep near the fire. Rye stared at the stars for hours before he finally fell asleep.

A rustle woke him. He pulled his pistol, pointing it at Otaktay. "Not too quiet, are you?" Rye said. Blanche woke up and slid behind Rye.

"You're still alive," Otaktay said. "I told my sister that you would not survive."

Rye looked at him, and his brow furrowed. "What do you want?"

Otaktay looked over at Blanche and then back at Rye. "I came to kill you and take that woman for my own. She will please me as long as I live."

A snide smile spread over Rye's face. "Won't happen."

"We will settle it in hand-to-hand combat now."

Rye thought for a second. He pulled up his pistol and shot him between the eyes. The chief dropped dead.

Blanche jumped at the shot. A scream came from behind the two of them.

"You killed him. You killed my brother."

Rye whipped around toward the voice.

Mina took two steps forward. "Have you no honor? It wasn't a fair fight. You are marked for death. The Sioux nation will hunt you for the remainder of your life. It will not matter where you go. As for her, she will be passed from warrior to warrior. Once the warriors are through with her, then she will be given to the women." Mina disappeared as quickly as she appeared.

Rye and Blanche looked at each other.

Rye looked at her with new eyes. He would keep her close. Blanche would lead him to the others. He sensed that Otaktay wouldn't have touched Blanche. But she would continue to use him. Two could play the game. He cinched the saddle, looked down at the dead warrior, and followed Blanche.

Chapter 12

With Rye feeling better, it meant the two could travel faster. After a couple of days of riding, they came across some unshod tracks. Indians in the area. The next day they found the body of a man shot full of arrows, scalped, and mutilated. Blanche had to turn her head away, even though she had seen much of this all before.

As they continued west, the air seemed drier and the temperature warmer. The land had little water. The wind became stronger making it difficult to breathe at times. Wind and heat slowed travel for the two. At the end of the day, they came upon a large river.

Neither Rye nor Blanche had been this far west, so they had no idea what to expect. They continued until they ran into a group of men camped on the river. Rye hesitated before riding in. Blanche touched him. "Be careful."

He nodded and hollered to the group. "We're coming in."

Blanche rode to the left of Rye. It would make it easier for Rye to fight if need be. She had seen his wicked speed with a pistol, even a better shot with the rifle.

Rye said under his breath, "I see six of them."

The men were ready for them, standing with hands near their holsters. Dangerous men who could handle any situation. Rye had seen men like these many times before.

A large bearded man stood in front of him with his rifle across his chest. "Looking for something?" he asked the two.

Rye responded, "Heading west. Wondering if you had a cup of coffee to spare and maybe some information you could provide."

"Nothing there but Indians and the wild. Sure you can handle it?"

Rye didn't say anything for a moment. "Know of any trading posts or a place where a person could get some goods?"

The big man looked at him and then at Blanche. He nodded his head toward the west. "Maybe a couple of days up the river from here, there's a trading post before you reach those hills yonder. They call it Fort Pierre."

"Thanks," Rye said. A voice stopped him as he turned the horse to move on.

"How do you expect to get across the river?"

"You told me Fort Pierre."

"I did, didn't I?"

"Are you sure you don't want to spend the night with us?" he paused and then smiled showing two missing front teeth. "Or maybe leave the pretty girl with us and you move on. We know how to handle a woman like that."

"I'm sorry. She's taken."

"By you?" said the man standing with the rifle.

"Yes, by me." Rye turned around once more and moved forward, nudging Blanche in front of him. At the click he swung around with his pistol and fired a shot that went through the man's skull, killing him instantly. "Who is next?"

No one moved. The two rode away in the direction the man had suggested before he died. Neither had talked the whole time. Rye finally stopped near a creek near a grove of trees. The tired duo crawled off the horses. Rye followed Blanche's every move. *Keep your enemies close* was his motto. She came back a few minutes later with some sticks and started a fire. Within moments she had supper ready.

"I could get used to this," Blanche broke the silence.

"Being near you out here on the prairie. It is so peaceful."

"I agree about peacefulness. But it is also dangerous. And it would be a question of who would kill the other first."

Blanche glared at him. "Did you have to kill him?"

"Yes."

"Thank you for saving my life, times three."

"I wasn't going to let them have you, Blanche."

She smiled at him. "You really don't know how amazing you are, do you?"

"What are you talking about?"

"Not once have you said anything about the death edict that Mina had cast upon us."

"What good does it do? Why haven't you said anything about it? You don't even act like you're scared."

"It is because I am with you. I have faith in you. You've been through so much in the past six months."

Rye stoked the fire, then took her hand, and led her away from the smoke. "We'll be safer over here."

"What about the horses?"

"I'm counting on them to give us a warning."

Rye sat against a tree, listening to the sound of the creek. The next morning the wind had picked up. Storm clouds had come in over the evening. A thunderstorm was rolling in on the horizon. He'd heard about torrential rains that could cause flash floods.

Rye decided to stay near the grove of trees until the storm went through. They prepared for the storm the best they could. The two quickly put together a patchwork lean-to. It wouldn't keep all the rain out, but it would give them some protection near the trees.

When the rains came, Rye and Blanche huddled together under a blanket inside the lean-to. The wind whipped through them. They couldn't stay dry amidst the wind and rain.

A crack of lightning spooked the horses. The noise and howling wind bore down on the shivering group. Rye scrambled from the blanket to grab the horses' reins. The mustang handled the storm much better than the horse Blanche rode.

Rye hobbled the horses near the trees. The downpour drenched and soaked each to their bones, but nothing could be done about it. The torrential rains caused the river waters to rise.

The bank collapsed throwing Blanche and Rye into the creek.

Blanche screamed as her head bobbed in the water. It took a few moments before Rye could reach Blanche and grab her from the river. He pulled the shivering woman close to him.

"Are you okay?"

"I am now," she said.

"We need to figure out a way to get you warm or you will catch pneumonia." Rye stripped her down to her undergarments, pulled a slicker off his horse, and put it on her. She pulled it tight around her. Rye rubbed her legs and arms the best he could. Another hour passed, then the rain subsided. The sun came out just like that.

Rye rushed to start a fire. It took time because of the wetness, but eventually he had a fire going. He moved Blanche as close to the fire as possible. With the clothes he had taken off her, he fanned the flames.

***

Blanche could feel the warmth coming back into her body. "You sure know how to show a girl a good time," she said.

Rye peered at her. "Are you feeling any better?

"Yes, I'm starting to warm up. Thank you."

He stared at her.

"What?" she asked.

"You are a beautiful woman. Looking at you like this, I see how beautiful you really are. Why are you blushing?"

"Oh I don't know. I just figure I'm like any other

woman."

Rye smiled at her. "I don't know about that. I can't remember ever seeing a woman look like you do half naked. Will you be okay while I find a way to get across the river?

She nodded.

***

Three men pulled up on their horses and stared at her. One of the men she'd seen with Marcus Duncan. Blanche smiled at him while she reached for the blanket and pulled it around her.

"No need to do that. You look much better without the blanket." He crawled off his horse and started toward her.

"Hold it, Bitter. Marcus Duncan said to bring her back unharmed."

He turned to look at the man on the horse. "Marcus isn't here now, is he?"

The man called Bitter leered at Blanche, then his face changed. She had a pistol pointed directly at him.

"Take one more step, and it will be your last one."

A chuckle somewhere behind her, then. "Bitter, I see she got the drop on you. What are you going to do about it?"

They turned at the voice. "She will shoot Bitter, and I will shoot the other two of you. Now slowly unbuckle your belts and drop them onto the ground."

Rye appeared from behind a grove of trees but remained on his horse. He kept his eyes on the three of them. Blanche gathered up their guns, being sure to stay out of their way.

"Captain Rye Tyler. Marcus Duncan will be glad to know you're still alive," the man called Bitter said.

Rye didn't answer him. He kept his eyes on the other two. "Howdy, Samuel. It's been a long time."

"It sure has, captain. We've been through a helluva lot, haven't we?"

"Do you know Tyler? Don't you know he's the man Marcus wants us to find and kill?"

"Yep, but like I told you and Marcus many times, he'll

be hard to kill. And at this moment he has the drop on us."

Rye spoke to Blanche, "Saddle up, and let's get out of here."

With a nod, she climbed on her horse and rode next to Rye.

"It looks like the young woman made a wise choice," Samuel said. "I always thought Blanche could do better than Raven."

He glanced at Blanche. "You are a fortunate woman. All Rye needed was someone to take care of him. If you stick with him, his fortunes will change."

She nodded at the man. He returned the nod.

Rye tied the other two men up to the tree, but left Samuel untied. "Give us an hour, Samuel, and then you can let those two loose to come after us. Before that I'll kill all of you." Rye stopped and turned to Samuel. "Why are you still with him?"

"Because I thought you were dead."

"All I want to do is be left alone. I'm heading away from civilization. Tell Marcus to leave me alone."

The two rode away.

"Do you trust him?"

Rye bit his lower lip. "No. It's just that he's not as evil as his brother."

"Will they come after us?"

"Yes, they will. But Samuel will keep his word, so that gives us time to move further west."

"Did you really mean it when you asked him to leave you alone?"

"Yes, I did."

"You will have to kill him, won't you?"

"I hope not."

Rye looked back toward where he had left the men. Then he found an easy route across the river where he and Blanche crossed. "We have an hour head start," he said. "Let's ride west."

They traveled for a week without any sign of white man or Indian. When they'd stopped to take a break at a large river, Rye turned back and looked toward the east. "No sign of anything," he said.

"Maybe they decided they had enough?"

"That's wishful thinking. Marcus Duncan is insane."

Blanche smiled.

Rye smiled back. "Even more insane than I am." He turned back to the river, needing to find an easy way to cross. Rye had heard of a settlement along the river up north a bit. He headed his horse in that direction. Blanche followed. An hour or so later, a cabin appeared in the distance sitting on the edge of the river. It also looked like the easiest place to cross. The two rode off the bluff. Rye tied Blanche's horse around his saddle horn and led the way across the river. They struggled but made it across. They took a break in silence.

Within an hour they headed west once more. In the distance loomed rugged, dry terrain. As they rode closer, the only landscape waiting for them were miles of mountainous rocks, eroded by wind and water.

Rye stopped the horses near the terrain. Steep slopes and very little vegetation.

"I have never seen anything like this," Blanche said.

Rye looked at her. "Neither have I. It looks very rugged. It may be a way to lose those who follow us."

Blanche gazed toward the east. She turned back to Rye.

He could tell she hoped someone would catch up with them. "I guess not. We can travel along the north side of the terrain. If trouble comes, we can hide in this rugged terrain. But this may be a good place to stop for the evening."

Rye crawled off his horse. He walked him through a tight squeeze and then up into a plateau. This place would be as good as any to camp for the night. The concealed area would make it difficult for anyone to reach them without them knowing.

Blanche started a fire. Rye fried some food. They sat and ate quietly, both thinking about other things.

Rye finally spoke up, "It may get colder up here, so it would be a good idea to snuggle into the blanket and stay closer to the fire."

"Thank you for thinking about me."

Rye looked at her, not sure how to respond, so he didn't. Blanche did as he suggested and soon was snoring. Rye didn't let himself fall asleep. He stayed alert to make sure no one had followed.

A coyote howled twice. Otherwise, quiet filled the air. Rye looked over at Blanche. Did she have any feelings for her sister, Libbie? From what he knew of her family, he doubted it. He finally fell asleep.

A couple of days later they saw what the Sioux called, 'Paha Sapa' or the whites called the Black Hills in the distance.

As they rode closer to the Black Hills, Blanche sighed at the sight. "This is beautiful."

"It truly is. One of the most beautiful places I've ever seen. I've heard Indians say the term, 'Paha Sapa.' It gives us a picture of their sacred mountains seen from a distance." They rode on. "The pines are called ponderosa pines. That is what gives the illusion of black from a distance. It also gives the illusion of the mountains emerging from the earth."

She stopped her horse and gazed at him. He stopped and glanced her way. "What?"

"You're a surprise to me." She started her horse west once more. This time Rye followed. They traveled most of the day. Midway through the afternoon, they saw a trading post with four horses tied to a stall outside the post.

Rye climbed off his horse and went to help Blanche down.

An old man sat in a rocking chair. "Can we help you?"

"We could use some food and some provisions."

He removed his glasses and studied them. "It looks like

you've come a long way."

"Yes we've come from the Dakota Territory," Rye responded.

"And you made it across without running into Sioux?"

"I never said that."

"You've been lucky."

"Why?" Blanche asked

"The Sioux are stirring up trouble all across Minnesota and the Dakota Territory. Where did you say you were heading?"

"We didn't," Rye said. "We're just looking for some provisions and then we will be on our way."

"I would recommend not heading any further west."

Blanche touched his shoulder. He turned to her. "I don't trust him, Rye," she said softly.

The old man looked at the two. "If you wish there is an area in the back with a bathtub to clean up."

Rye and Blanche stepped inside. While waiting for Blanche to take a bath, Rye chatted with the old man. All the talk revolved around the Rocky Mountains.

"How long would it take to reach the Rocky Mountains?"

"It's a good week from here if you're lucky. And with a young woman, it could be even tougher."

"She can handle her own."

"I hope so because you are going to get your fill of Sioux, Shoshone, and Crow. I also heard some Blackfeet have been seen around."

Rye nodded and walked back into the settler's store. Blanche had finished her bath and stood by herself trying on a blue dress. She had just zipped up the back when Rye walked over. "You look good in that dress," Rye said.

"Thank you. It actually fits. They don't make a lot of dresses my size."

"Well, this one fits you just right."

"You could do with a bath yourself." She held her finger

under her nose and winked.

He pulled the curtain and took off his clothes, then climbed into the tub and lowered himself into it. The water soothed him.

As he soaked, Rye thought about Blanche Park. She sure didn't seem like the woman she portrayed. She looked more sophisticated than any woman he had met. That woman had style. He also knew she hadn't told him everything and probably wouldn't. She knew Marcus Duncan and knew him well.

A few moments later, he climbed out of the tub, dried himself off, and put on his clothes. He walked out into the main area. Blanche was browsing the shelves for needed items. She had taken the dress off and slipped into riding clothes.

Once she completed her shopping and purchased everything that they'd need, they climbed on their horses and headed west once again. This time they included heavy coats and boots for the trek into the mountains.

***

The old man stared after the two. Something about them didn't seem right. He wanted the beautiful woman, and he always got what he wanted. He'd give them a couple of hours' lead and then he and his men would follow along. That woman would be his tonight.

***

The two journeyed slowly west. Blanche noticed Rye deep in thought and asked him about it.

"The old man doesn't fit the mold."

"What do you mean?"

"If there were that many Indian concerns out here, why didn't he stop us? We had better be on the lookout for that old geezer."

She frowned at him. He went on. "Where did you get all the money?"

"You forget I come from a rich family." She could see

the hurt in his face as soon as the words came out. Another layer of this complicated man emerged. He had pride. But truth be known, she didn't care what he thought about her money.

***

They rode for another hour or two before they decided to make camp along a riverbed. Neither had any idea where they were. But it didn't matter because Rye knew they needed to stop.

After the fire was going and they were eating supper, Rye spoke up, "It may be a long night. Those men aren't going to let us get out of here. They will come for you."

Blanche peered at him. "Then I guess we'd better be ready." She threw some more sticks onto the fire, while Rye brought both horses away from the fire. He gathered what he could to provide them shelter, then motioned for Blanche to sit between a pile of logs, and he handed her a rifle. Then he plopped down next to her with another one.

"Make as many shots count as you can. If not, I'll have to hunt them down in the dark. Whenever that happens, stay between the horses for some shelter and always be prepared."

"I will."

***

The men at the trading post finally caught up with them. They slowed down when the fire drew them toward the grove of trees.

Soon that woman would be his. He'd use her and then slit her throat. The old man didn't care what happened to the man with her. That would be up to the other three men in the group, all renegades like himself.

The men who followed him knew how he operated and also knew that they'd get what they wanted. They made their move after the fire dimmed in the camp. Inching into the camp, they poured lead into Rye's body. The old man at the trading post swore in disgust when he discovered it wasn't him.

***

A bullet plugged the old geezer in the head. Then a second and third fell right after. One turned and ran toward the horses located at the water's edge.

Rye stepped out from the river and shot him point-blank in the chest. The man fell into the water. "It's okay, Blanche, they're all dead. You can come out."

Blanche led the horses out with her. "Can we leave this place now?"

"What?" Rye frowned at her.

"Please, let's leave this place now."

Rye couldn't understand her thinking. She crawled onto her horse, and Rye climbed up on his. They quietly headed west in the dark.

Chapter 13

In mid-September, when Rye and Blanche rode into the western area of the Dakota Territory, the weather had turned colder. The wind blew strong for the few days that they made their trek across the territory. Neither knew anything about the Rocky Mountains.

As they moved along the trail, Rye described all the wild animals like pronghorn deer, elk, and bear.

"How do you know so much about the wildlife out here?"

"I do know how to read."

Blanche laughed.

Again, like the Black Hills, the details of the mountain enthralled Blanche. She enjoyed the many different colors of flowers that made them look beautiful. Unlike the Black Hills, the snow-covered peaks capped the Rockies in the distance.

She couldn't wait until they reached them to enjoy their beauty up close. They continued traveling higher, much higher than the Black Hills. The mountain's layers looked more rugged and lonely. She figured Rye desired the loneliness, but the trap had been set the moment he rode into the mountains.

She glanced up when Rye stopped suddenly. He swung around pulling out his pistol. Standing not fifty feet away were four Sioux Indians. Blanche touched Rye's arm.

One of the Sioux was talking in his native tongue.

Neither she nor Rye could speak the Sioux language. Blanche remembered Mina's prophecy. Nothing good could come from this.

The Sioux sat on their horses in a row. Rye moved his horse forward pulling Blanche's beside him.

"What are you doing?"

"Taking a chance. Whatever you do, do not look at them. Keep your eyes looking forward."

She did as he asked. He slowly walked his horse toward them. The Sioux stared at the white man and woman coming toward them.

When Rye stopped in front of them, he motioned to them to part.

One said something to the man sitting next to him in the Sioux language. He answered in the same tongue, then he turned to Rye and Blanche. "He says you should both die."

"We would not be the only ones to die. There will be your blood also."

For a moment they looked at him, and then all of a sudden, the two middle ones parted.

Rye moved forward with Blanche at his side through the gap they'd created.

Once past, the Sioux spoke in English once more. "You are as brave as Mina said you would be." The Sioux yelled and came charging after them.

Rye swung his horse around keeping him between the Sioux and Blanche. He fired two shots killing the two lead Sioux. "Ride, Blanche, ride. I'm right behind you."

Blanche and Rye bolted away with two warriors after them on the trail. As they rounded the bend, four more warriors sat on the trail. Rye stopped quickly. When he did his horse tumbled down the hill on top of him.

Blanche screamed. She spurred her horse down after him. Despite the rough terrain, Blanche knew how to handle a horse. Rye had jumped off the Black and rolled down the hill. He looked up and saw Blanche coming down and the

Sioux looking down on them.

Rye jumped up, pulled up the Black, and shouted at Blanche, "Go, Blanche. Head out toward the open. Maybe we can put some distance between us."

By this time, the Sioux had made it down the hill and were gaining on them.

"Do you trust me?"

"Yes, with my life," Blanche said.

"Rein in the horse."

She did just that.

"Get off quick. Grab the water and the rifle."

She did as he asked. He jumped off right behind her and laid the horse down in front of them. He swatted the Black, and the horse ran away.

"Get behind the horse and make every shot count."

The Sioux came riding past them. Rye shot one of the warriors and Blanche missed her shots. They turned around and came from the other side. Rye pulled Blanche over the top of the horse. They fired from the other side. This time each killed a couple of Sioux.

The Sioux stopped for a moment to gather their bearings. Rye's shoulders slumped. He was beat. Blanche touched his shoulder, and he looked up.

"You are the strongest person I know, Rye. Please pull it together."

He smiled at her. "If something should happen to me, take the pistol." He stopped.

"I know what to do. Nothing will happen."

Rye studied the Sioux as he loaded his rifle. Four left.

"What are you doing?" Blanche asked.

"You said you trusted me."

"Yes, I do."

"Okay, be prepared."

The howling started as all four came racing toward them on their Indian ponies. Within fifty yards from them, Rye stood and walked towards them.

Blanche screamed at him, "What are you doing?"

They came galloping toward him. He calmly put a bullet in the first, then the second, and each one fell before they reached within ten yards of him. His rifle jammed as the last warrior came up on him, ready to shoot an arrow through him. Rye fell to the ground.

The only Sioux alive stopped a few yards away and spoke to him in English, "You will not live." He spun his horse around and raced away. Rye lifted his rifle, pulled, and knocked the warrior off the horse. It took a moment to realize that Blanche was next to him.

She smacked him on the arm. "What are you doing? Trying to get yourself killed?" Tears streamed down her face, and she started talking. He listened.

"At the age of twelve, I saw my mother and father murder a man for no reason. They told me it involved a feud with your family. I have hated the Tylers and Davises ever since then."

Rye didn't believe a word she said. She went on. "You came along, and they told me you needed to die. But then I saw you. You were not the man I expected. I can't explain it except you care about others. I want everyone in your family dead, but not you. Now all we're doing is fighting for our lives. What were you thinking?"

"Guess I wasn't thinking. I just reacted."

"Are you totally insane?' she asked him. "Are you trying to get killed?"

His lips curved up.

"What is so funny?" she asked.

"I didn't think you cared about me as much as you do."

She frowned at him for a moment. "Rye, you really don't know how bad Butler Lily wants you dead. Now you have the whole Sioux nation after us. It won't stop until you're dead. I don't know if I can handle them butchering you." He put his arm around her, pulled her down to sit on the grass, and kissed the top of her head.

After a few moments, she let out a big sigh. "I guess we should do something besides sitting here waiting for more Sioux to come back."

Rye got up. She reached up her hand and he pulled her up. Both looked at the horse. Three arrows stuck out of him.

Rye looked at Blanche and then looked to the West. He turned back to her. "Do you feel like going for a bit of a hike?"

She nodded and took his hand. "Why not? We don't have much else to do."

"That's my girl."

She stopped. "Where is the Black?"

"He'll catch up with us when he's ready."

***

Rye pulled off the saddle and slung it over his shoulder. The two headed toward the mountain pass in the distance. Rye stopped after taking only three steps. He stared at the mountains. Blanche looked there also.

More Sioux warriors sat on one of the buttes. The two looked at each other.

"Hell of a walk," Rye commented. Blanche burst out laughing.

"What the hell," he responded.

She grabbed his hand and they headed toward the closest cover. Rye kept his eyes averted from the Sioux, but he knew where they were.

Moments later, they let out a yell and went screaming down the hill toward Rye and Blanche.

"We'd better hurry, Rye. They're getting awfully close."

Rye didn't say anything but started to quicken his pace. Blanche did the same. Twenty yards from a group of rocks, Rye said, "Run toward the rocks."

She did. When the first few Indians got close to them, they dove behind the rocks. Rye quickly turned around and nailed one of the Indians with his pistol as shots pinged against the rocks.

The two continued firing at the Sioux. The fight lasted for another hour before the Indians moved out of Rye's rifle range. Rye counted at least four dead Indians, but plenty more were still living. The stoic warriors sat on their horses staring at the rocks.

"What is happening, Rye?"

"I haven't a clue. They could wipe us out if they wanted to. We don't have many bullets left. What I don't understand is where they got the guns?"

"Butler Lily."

Rye peered at her.

"Butler has been selling weapons to the Sioux, Crow, and Blackfeet. My guess is he and his crew are somewhere nearby."

"He's not going to let us have any peace."

Neither one said anything. Blanche finally spoke up, "In my heart I know we will find a way out of this. You always seem to have an answer."

Rye glanced over at the Sioux sitting on their horses, not moving. He gazed down at Blanche who snuggled into him. He didn't know why but he held her tightly. "Not only are you beautiful, you're also athletic."

She tapped him on the shoulder. "Probably because I've been chasing you for eleven years."

Both remained silent.

"Do you remember much about your childhood?"

"No, I don't," Rye responded.

"That's too bad."

Rye took Blanche's hands. "You are not an everyday country girl. You have class and sophistication. But you didn't get that from your family."

"When I went to school back east, I didn't want to come back."

"Why did you?"

"Butler Lily."

"What?"

"I found out he paid my way through school, so I owed him. He and my father used me to acquire land from others. Like you, many in the valley felt the same way about my beauty. My father used my looks as a way to become more powerful."

She stared out into the distance. "You have to realize something. I am part of the plan to destroy you. That all changed that day when you found me in the slough. You melted my heart right then and there...for the second time in my life. The first time, at ten, I felt the same way. You actually kissed me one time on the cheek."

Voices. Rye gently moved Blanche to the side and peered out where the Sioux had been. They had disappeared. Rye stood and pulled Blanche up. "I have no idea what happened," he said. "Let's take advantage of our good fortune and move to a safe place."

They walked for at least three hours before coming to a river. Rye stopped. The crude map Rye had picked up at the trading post labeled it as the Belle Fourche River. More importantly, it provided some shelter.

He dropped the saddle in a grove of trees. Blanche quickly gathered some branches for a fire.

"I think it may snow," she said.

"It is cold enough."

"What are you planning?"

"Right now I'm going to get a fire going to build up some heat. We have a couple of days left, and we should go to our destination."

"Why did you head west?"

Rye stirred the fire thinking about how to respond. "I'm not necessarily sure why I wanted to come west. Mostly I'm just tired of fighting. I want some peace for myself."

"Why out here? This seems so wild."

Rye said, "I'm hoping to make a fresh start with my life. Why didn't you head back east?"

"Because you're here. Until you tell me to go away or

pass me off to a safe place, I'll be right with you."

Rye fried some of the beans they had picked up at the trading post. A few moments later, the two quietly ate their supper. It had been a long day. They fell asleep on either side of the fire.

The next morning Rye woke up, got a fire going, and fried some bacon. Blanche looked at him half awake, but smiling.

"What are you smiling about?"

"The bacon smells so good."

After breakfast the two headed toward the mountains.

Suddenly, Rye burst out laughing.

"What's so funny?"

"This saddle. I think I've carried it more than it's been on the back of a horse."

"You do have a sense of humor, and it especially shows when we are in danger."

Within a few hours, the two reached another river. Rye pulled out the crude map and studied it. "This must be the Powder River. If my calculations are correct, we should be to the Bighorns sometime tomorrow."

"I can't wait," Blanche said, a big smile on her face. They gazed to the west at the mountains springing up before them. So dark, even darker than the Black Hills a week or so earlier. "Why do they look so dark?" Blanche asked.

"It's the way the sun is hitting them."

"They look mysterious."

"That they do."

Rye stopped and looked at her. "Maybe we shouldn't have drifted this way."

Blanche hesitated for a moment before responding, "I feel safe with you. I have always felt safe with you even through everything we've gone through."

Rye laughed.

"What?"

"After all we've been through, you feel safe being with

me? That's hard to imagine after everything I've put you through. Indians one day. Crazy men another day. Who knows what's next?"

"Whatever comes upon us, I know in my heart you'll find a way through it."

He stopped and quickly put his fingers to his lips. "That could be sooner than you think. This way," he said quietly. They ducked into a gully and waited. Above them Sioux warriors rode past in a single file. At least a dozen. All painted for war. They waited silently until they left.

"Where do you think they're heading?"

"I don't know," Rye responded. Before Blanche could say another word, Rye added, "I think they're scouting the area for us." Rye led the way down the gully to search for another way out. About fifteen minutes later, they emerged into an opening and headed north toward a grove of trees below a hill. "We'd better get underneath some cover. This should protect us from anyone else seeing us and allow us to see what is happening."

Blanche turned to move away.

Don't wander too far away."

"Okay."

Chapter 14

Blanche gathered sticks and thought about everything that had transpired. A strong hand went around her mouth, and she struggled to break away. Blanche finally got a chance to see who had taken her by force. "Hi, Marcus." she smiled.

"Hi, Blanche," her father said. "I see you finally fulfilled your part of the bargain and brought the man we've been hunting to us."

She smiled. "I did."

***

Rye searched around for Blanche.

"Don't think about it, Tyler."

He turned slowly. Butler Lily pointed a gun at him. "I'd just as soon pull the trigger right now, but I told a friend of both of ours that I would turn you over to him for safekeeping." He paused and then added, "Why didn't you just die when you were shot?"

Rye stared at him without flinching.

"Hand over your gun to Brandt. You won't need it where you're going."

Butler motioned him to move. He headed toward the direction that Blanche had walked. He walked for about ten minutes when he came upon the camp hidden in the rocks.

Rye slumped down to the ground. He didn't know what to believe about any of this. They brought Blanche over to him and pushed her to the ground.

"Another fine mess you got us into, Rye." Blanche said and then smiled.

Rye looked at her. Then Libbie walked over to them.

"Rye Tyler, this wouldn't have been so painful if you would have joined us in our adventure. As for you, Blanche, you always seem to fall for the wrong kind of man. It won't matter after tomorrow. It will be a reunion of sorts for you."

Libbie locked eyes with Rye, then walked away, leaving Blanche and him alone.

Rye felt those eyes were trying to tell him something. She left. Voices. Rye counted at least twenty men along with Price Davis and his wife and Libbie.

Libbie brought some food to them. "Just like old times, Blanche. Remember when you were younger, and I had to feed you when you became sick? Now look at you. You chose to hitch your coattails to a deserter and a coward."

Libbie fed them and then left.

Blanche gazed at Rye. "You're not a coward. Like I said before, you are the bravest man I've ever known. I have faith that we'll get out of this alive."

Rye didn't respond. He stared at the group of men hanging around the fire. At least twice he noticed Libbie staring at him with that same look in her eyes. One by one, they stood and turned in for the night. Blanche had fallen asleep.

Around midnight, all but one guard fell asleep. The man passed by Rye.

"Can I get up and take care of business?" Rye asked.

The man nodded for him to get up. He walked with him to the woods out of sight.

"Unless you want to help me out, I'm going to need the ropes off my wrists."

The man hesitated. He then untied Rye's wrists.

As soon as he did that, Rye whipped around and broke his neck. He turned at a soft voice. "What are you doing here, Libbie?"

"I don't know. I'm terrified of what is happening, especially what is happening to you."

He took her hand and pulled her toward him, kissing her on the lips. She responded to the kiss with passion. Then she backed off. The kiss had taken her breath away. "Please don't. You must go. They will kill you."

"I can't. Not until I end it all. Please come with me?"

She gazed into his eyes. "I want to, but it is better for both of us if I stay where I am."

Rye turned to go. Libbie touched him once more. "You have to go back and get Blanche. You need her to survive, for now. But don't trust her."

Rye smiled at Libbie. "What? You are the only one I can ever trust. I can't believe how, even in the dark, I can feel your slender, athletic body against mine. It feels good. And I don't believe your breasts have gotten any bigger than when we were kids."

"Rye Tyler, they are fine breasts. They're just smaller than most. I will tell you this. Even in the dark I noticed your rugged, handsome face. Of course, in the cabin, despite your shaggy look, you have toned up well."

Neither knew what to say to the other. Finally, Libbie smiled. "That darn Black of yours is up the trail waiting for you. I have no idea why, but he just showed up one day. I kept him knowing you would be coming."

"Thanks, Libbie. Please take care of yourself."

"I want you to know that I have always loved you and have never stopped."

"Forget me. No one will ever know that I have any connection to you—ever." He grabbed the rifle and his pistol belt and crept back toward Blanche. Rye knelt down by the woman, shaking her and putting his finger to his lips. He helped her up, and they slipped quietly out of the camp. Once out of sight, he untied her ropes.

Blanche put her arms around him and kissed him on the lips.

"Why did you do that?"

"Did you plan to leave us?"

Both stopped at the voice. Rye recognized it. "Sergeant Marcus Duncan."

"It's been awhile, Captain Tyler. Take both of them back to Lily."

Walking back to Lily's camp, Duncan spoke up, "Got a beauty here, Captain. I'm surprised. She must not know who you are."

He smiled at her. "I'm heartbroken, Blanche. You were promised to me."

Blanche started to say something but felt Rye squeeze her arm slightly. She didn't say anything.

Back at camp, Duncan said, "Well, Sergeant, you'd best keep a closer eye on your captives. You should have known that Tyler would escape. He's slipped through enemy lines several times in the war."

Lily didn't say anything. One of Duncan's men spoke up. "And he has a real beauty with him. Maybe he would share her?"

"Bitter, you'd better watch it around that woman. She may just cut your gizzard in your sleep," Duncan said. "If the captain is with her, that means he cares about her. And the man, as you know, doesn't care about anyone."

Price Davis walked up. "Lily, is this the man we've been expecting?"

"Yes sir."

Davis sized him up. "This is the man who's going to help us win the West? Doesn't seem like much."

Duncan chuckled. "Well, Captain, do you want to tell him, or would you like me to?" With a flick of his wrist, Duncan sliced off Price Davis's right ear. The man screamed.

He pulled Davis up and looked him in the face. "Do you think that will do?" He pushed him aside.

"Blanche, don't you remember you were promised to

me? Now you are with the man I've wanted to destroy. Things are different now. What do you think of that, Captain?"

Rye didn't answer.

"No matter. No one here will harm the woman...at least not yet." Before he could finish his sentence, Rye whipped him around, grabbed his pistol out of his holster, and pointed it at his head. "Tell them to back off, Duncan, or I will spill your brains here and now. I probably will die, but I'll take many with me."

Duncan nodded at the others.

Rye motioned at Blanche, who grabbed a rifle and pistol, then dropped to the ground. "Go, Blanche. Move quickly."

Libbie smiled at Blanche. Rye saw it. An evil smile. But why?

Rye dragged Duncan away from the others. Price glared at Butler Lily. "Kill the son of a bitch."

Nobody moved.

Rye had pinned Duncan against a tree. "Blanche, let's move." He whispered in Duncan's ear. "Don't come after me or I will kill you. And don't even think about harming Blanche. I'll hunt you down if anything happens to her."

"If anything happens to me, those three kids you adore will die at the hands of the Sioux or maybe the Blackfeet. If I recall correctly, you are on the Sioux's most wanted list."

"What?"

"Oh, to be clear, Captain Tyler, the game is just beginning. You will do as I say, or those three children whom you seem to care about won't survive. It won't be pleasant."

"I guess that is something we'll have to discuss at a later date." With that Rye hit him on the side of the head with his pistol. He glanced at Blanche. "Everything will be on foot for now. Our best bet is into the Bighorns. Hopefully, we can make it by morning to give us some protection."

They didn't talk but hurried through the trees and then

out into the plains. Even in the dark, the majestic view of the mountains loomed before them.

"We have a long walk ahead of us." Rye said. They trudged along the open area in the dark. "Do you think he told the truth about having the kids?"

"Knowing Duncan, yes."

"Why didn't you go back for those kids?"

"I'm not sure where he has them. That is something that will have to be dealt with on another day. He won't harm them." She glanced at him. "He should be afraid of you. You're wicked with a rifle or pistol, and just now you were like greased lightning."

"That is the educated girl I know speaking. Did you ever figure out what you wanted to do with that degree?"

"I wasn't sure what I wanted to do, but I knew I wanted something more than living on a farm."

"Now look at what is happening."

"Things change. Like I said earlier, my father—and I later found out—Butler Lily helped pay for my education from the money stolen from the Sioux. When I returned last year, they wanted the money paid back. Needless to say, I couldn't do that, so they made an arrangement."

"So, what kind of education did you get?"

"I took business classes."

"That's nice. Do you plan on becoming that financial wizard you'd thought about earlier?"

"Don't know yet."

"I'm sure something will come up. The first thing is getting out of this mess."

"We're still alive, so that's a start."

"That we are."

"How did you know Duncan?"

"He and I were in an elite group. He systematically killed all the others in the group after Jefferson Davis sent me on my own to spy for the Confederates."

"So that's what he meant about going in and out of

lines."

"Yep."

Blanche stopped and took Rye's hand. "I love you, Rye Tyler." She kissed him on the lips.

"We will find the kids, and we will get them back."

Blanche smiled and the two continued walking.

***

Marcus Duncan threw things around the campfire. "That man will die one way or another. I don't care. And the woman will wish the Sioux had caught her before I do. I think she's fallen for the man."

Samuel looked at his older brother. He didn't tell his brother that she had wanted her also. All he said. "We don't have the kids."

"What the hell happened?"

No one said anything. Samuel spoke up. "Members of the wagon train kept them."

Butler Lily spoke up, "What are you thinking?"

"I'm thinking the man can't survive out there. He has nowhere to go. We're trailing him, and there are different tribes of Indians in those mountains he will have to get through."

Marcus Duncan stood staring toward the west. "I just hope I'm there to see the Indians butcher him, or even better, put a bullet into his forehead myself."

***

Rye and Blanche struggled toward the mountains. A couple of times they stopped to catch their breath.

"What I don't understand is why you are going to the Bighorns."

He hesitated a moment gathering his thoughts. "I'm a deserter, and many people are chasing me. There is a reward for my head, not only from Lily, but from the Confederate Army. I felt the West and the mountains would be the easiest places to get lost." He smiled at her. "Now answer me a question. Why are you sticking so close to me and putting yourself in this kind of danger?"

"For a bright boy, you can be stupid sometimes, Rye Tyler. I told you once I fell in love with you the first time I met you. I always will...even if you don't feel the same way about me."

The sun was rising when they reached the edge of the mountains.

"Man, these are beautiful," he said and rested an arm around her shoulders.

Chapter 15

Rye and Blanche started the climb up the mountain. They reached a spot that provided shelter from the weather and shelter from those chasing them. They could see a distance around them. No doubt Butler Lily and Marcus Duncan would be coming. They needed Rye for something, or Lily would have killed him immediately. It would also be a matter of pride. Rye and Blanche had escaped from right under their noses.

"Let's hole up here for now. Try to get some sleep, and I'll keep watch."

"No, Rye, you get some sleep. You need it more than I do. We'll need your strength to get through this. And sleep is important to you right now."

She took the rifle from him and sat down near a rock where she would be hidden but had a panoramic view. Blanche turned around a moment later, and Rye had fallen asleep. She smiled to herself. She could just as well end it here. His brother wouldn't want that; he wanted to be the one doing the killing. She knew now she couldn't pull the trigger even if she was asked. Blanche was overwhelmed by the beauty and was falling in love with this place. The mountains rose up majestically. Above them a small creek flowed into a basin.

Rye finally woke up.

"Get a nice sleep?" Blanche said, smiling at him.

"I sure did. I feel rested. How about yourself?"

"I'm enjoying the beauty."

Rye stepped over near her. "It is beautiful, isn't it?"

"I can see why you wanted to settle out here." "See anything out there?"

"Haven't seen a thing. But they wouldn't know which direction we traveled."

"My guess is the Indian trackers are already on our scent and will find us soon enough."

"Do you think they would just give up if they didn't find us and go on to their next great adventure?"

"Don't think so. For Butler Lily, it's all about getting even with me no matter how long it takes. Marcus Duncan is a completely different story. Right now, we have to find something to eat." Rye headed up the mountain a bit.

"Where are you going?"

"To find something to eat."

Blanche stood and started to follow him.

"Where are you going?" he asked.

"With you. Last time we separated, I got us into a pickle. I'm not going to let that happen again."

"Let's do it," he said taking the rifle from her.

The higher they climbed, the more they could see around them. Rye pointed toward a dust cloud several miles away. He looked to the north and saw the same.

"It looks like they're spreading out, checking for signs. Sooner or later they'll find the trek we took into the mountains." Rye stared at the mountain above them. "Hopefully we can make it over the top of this peak before they find us. Once that happens, we'll have the advantage."

She looked down the mountain. They struggled to climb it. He stopped when something moved. A mountain goat. A shot wouldn't do because those down below would hear the noise from the rifle.

They moved on. It became more difficult the higher they climbed, not only from the energy they exerted, but also from the altitude, which drained them as they climbed higher, especially for Blanche.

"Let's stop here. We need to find some food or we won't be able to climb anymore. Water would help also."

"Listen," Blanche said.

Rye heard it also. "It sounds like a waterfall."

They followed the sound to the waterfall in the distance. They also saw the Black staring at Rye. "I'll be damned," he said.

Blanche threw her arms around Rye. "We did it." She led the way down to the waterfall and found a pond sitting to the left of the waterfall. Rye knelt down and took a cup of water in his hands. He drank some more before he had his fill.

***

Unknown to them sat an Indian hidden in the trees across the pond staring at them. He didn't come in for the kill. He'd head back to the village to bring others. The brave slipped back into the forest.

***

Rye saw what looked like a sage grouse. He hesitated to take a shot, but they needed food. He aimed and nailed the bird as it took off. It fell near the pond. He raced over to grab it. "Come on, Blanche, we have to find a place to hide, build a fire, and cook this." He scanned the area and saw an opening into the mountains. "Over there." They scrambled up the mountainside into a small clearing. Rye took the Black's reins. Blanche grabbed the grouse.

"This will do. It looks like a trail used by Indians and wild game. It doesn't look like it's been used for a while."

"Good because I'm starved."

"You grab the sticks, and I'll skin the bird."

A few minutes later, Rye had a fire going and the bird cooked through. Rye tore a piece and handed it to Blanche. She hesitated before eating it.

"What?"

"Nothing, I'm just thinking about finally putting

something into my stomach," she said hesitating.

"Well, don't look at the bird, eat it," Rye responded.

Blanche smiled and picked at her portion. Rye sat and tore off another piece for him. Once finished, Rye and Blanche started down the trail to the waterhole. The Indian rode out of the grove of trees, intersecting their path.

"Get down out of sight," Rye whispered. They had nowhere to go. He hoped the Indian would just move on. Rye tried to communicate with the Indian, but the Indian didn't understand a word he said. The Indian pulled out his knife and lunged toward Rye. Rye didn't have a knife. He lifted his rifle and plugged him in the chest.

Rye hurried to the horse before it got spooked. The Indian's horse had a water pouch and a bow with arrows. He took the horse toward the Indian, grabbed the knife lying next to its owner, and turned him over. The warrior's tribe was a mystery. It didn't matter. What he did know was they had to get out of there.

Too late, the other warriors rode into view.

He pulled the horse up the trail. It didn't struggle, which made Rye think the horse had traveled through the mountains. Rye made it to the top of the group of rocks where Blanche stood with the Black. "Are you okay?" he asked.

She stared at him. "I'm just glad you're okay. I counted at least a dozen Indians down there."

"I guess this is as good a place to make a stand as any."

It didn't matter what either of them felt because the Indians rushed toward them screaming at the top of their lungs. One reached close to the bottom of the trail and crawled up the rest of the way. Rye shot him with the bow and arrow.

"Ah ... proficient with a bow and arrow also. Your skills never cease to amaze me," Blanche said smiling.

"I don't have many shells left in the rifle. I want to make them last as long as possible. The pistol is only good at close range."

The Indians fired at will with rifles. Blanche and Rye looked at each other, knowing where the rifles had come from. They stayed down to keep from being hit by the barrage of rifle shots ricocheting through the rocks.

The shooting stopped. Rye heard something to his left, and just as an Indian came out into the open, Rye shot him in the chest. He screamed and fell. Rye gathered all the weapons, which included a rifle and a knife. The Indian also left a carton of rifle shells. "This will help immensely," he said.

Blanche peered at Rye. "I take it that means they all will be armed with an arsenal of weapons."

"Yep."

The two kept their eyes peeled. Everything seemed quiet. They both knew appearances were merely that. They had killed two for sure, and Blanche had spotted at least a dozen when it all started.

Blanche spoke quietly, "They won't give up, will they?"

"From what I know about Indians, they love the sport of hunting. I have no idea what tribe we're dealing with here. Shoshone, but I'm not sure."

Shadows were eating up the daylight.

"With the sun setting, will it help us?" Blanche asked.

"I don't know. My feeling is they won't give up. Climb on to the horse and we'll feel our way down the other side until we come to a place where we can safely defend." He helped Blanche on the horse, then climbed on the Black.

They headed slowly down the mountain trail. Blanche's horse excelled in this terrain, which helped them. They traveled for an hour, the darkness enveloping them. The cold and wind set in, and snow started to spit.

"We've got to find a place to hole up," Rye said.

Blanche pointed to an area with coverage, which would allow them to get off the trail. Rye pushed aside the brush; inside was a place to hide and keep warm.

"Can we light a fire?" she asked.

"We'll need one to keep us warm. Go ahead and light a small one."

He led the horses to a corner of the rocks out of the way. There also happened to be a blanket on the horse Blanche rode to help stay warm in the night. After that he returned to Blanche. "No matter how you look at it, we're in trouble," he said. "We have the weather to deal with. We have Butler Lily, Marcus Duncan, and your father chasing us. We have that Indian tribe out to kill us. If that's not enough, I'm a deserter, and the Confederacy will be after me."

"A piece of cake."

"What?"

"I know that we're in trouble, but we'll get through it somehow," she said, pulling him down near her. "You need to warm up, or none of those things will matter anyway."

He wrapped the blanket around the two of them. It wasn't long before Blanche drifted off to sleep. Rye dozed off not long after.

His eyes snapped open. He thought he had heard something. Rye quickly moved Blanche out of the way and crept to the front of the bushes. A different group of Indians than last night's rode past. War paint covered their faces, their eyes darting back and forth on the trail. One stopped and stared Rye's way. A Cheyenne Dog Soldier—the first he'd seen. Rye had heard how deadly they were. All the Indian tribes, including the Sioux, avoided them when they could.

For some reason the soldier didn't stop to take a closer look at the bushes Rye and Blanche hid behind. He counted about fifteen warriors riding by. The Black remained quiet. Rye scurried back to the pony and covered his muzzle.

Rye stayed silent for what seemed at least ten minutes. Blanche had joined him and touched his arm. He put a finger to his lips. The last of the warriors rode by. They waited until the Dog Soldiers had ridden out of sight.

"What do we do now?" she asked.

"We'll give them some time, and then we'll head off to the west to find a place to hide."

Chapter 16

"Where the hell could they have gone?" Butler Lily asked no one in particular.

"They're up there somewhere in the mountains. My guess is the Indians got them, or maybe they fell into a deep crevice. Who knows?" Price Davis shrugged.

Butler turned around to look at Davis. Marcus Duncan and his men had taken a different route into the mountains to hunt Tyler down. Butler Lily and his men had tried to go from the north.

Libbie comforted him. "Come on now, Butler. Maybe it's time to forget about him and move toward our ultimate goal—the silver mines in Montana. More money for everyone."

"That's what I'm talking about," another of his men said. "Besides it's getting too damn cold here, and we need to head to a place with plenty of whiskey and women."

"Guess you're right. Let's head north," Lily said.

Davis nodded. He had already sent his wife and others up north. He couldn't figure out why Libbie didn't join them.

Marcus Duncan and his men came to an area where a battle had obviously taken place. Two dead Indians. It seemed unusual that the dead weren't claimed. That could only mean they had problems of their own. His scouts came back after checking out the area and told Marcus Duncan that the Shoshone rode over the mountain. One had found the trail. He also said two others had been up there fighting them.

"Tyler is still alive. Let's head over the mountain. At least we found the direction they've gone."

The man called Bitter walked over to Duncan. "Do you think they're heading toward the shack?"

Marcus Duncan didn't say anything for a moment. "Captain Tyler would know nothing about a shack up here in the mountains, but that's a good possibility. We'll head that way." He turned to Samuel who was frowning at him.

"You don't know who you are dealing with?"

He smiled at his little brother, then turned back to everyone. "Let's move."

***

Up in the Bighorn Mountains, Rye and Blanche struggled to climb the mountains. Light snow continued, but to the west, the sky looked ominous.

"It looks like we could be in for a big snowstorm," Blanche said as the two walked alongside each other.

"It's getting colder too. We need to find shelter, or we will not survive. A blizzard is on its way."

Blanche sighed. She couldn't understand the logic of staying with him, but here she was, walking next to him. All the odds were stacked against them. Their only advantage was the rifle and shells taken off the Indian. She also knew that this man had defied many odds over the past few months, in fact, the past few years. Maybe she was on the wrong side of it all.

They traveled on foot for another hour. The snow became heavier, making it tougher to see in front of them. There'd been no other Indian tracks or signs of anybody.

"We should climb on the horses and ride some. You probably need some rest."

She nodded.

Both climbed on the horses and headed down the trail, with no idea where it led. They rode for a distance until they saw a building. Maybe a cabin of some sort. If so, there may be people inside.

"Here, take the horse's reins and give me the rifle."

Blanche did as he asked. They slowly walked toward the structure. As they got closer, the structure turned out to be a cabin. A refuge that would save them.

Rye hollered, "Anybody in the cabin?" No one answered.

They walked a little closer.

"What's that in front?" Blanche asked.

It looked like a body. Rye gripped his rifle, ready to fire if need be. Once they reached the body, Rye rolled it over. Scalped. Blanche jumped back at the sight.

"It's okay, Blanche. It looks like he's been dead for a few days."

"Was it the group of Indians we saw earlier today?"

"I don't know. Possibly. Let's see what's inside." He walked toward the cabin and pushed open the door. The room included a stove, bed, and food. Two weapons leaned against the wall. Others had been here recently.

Rye dragged the man around back. He took the horses to an area on the side out of the wind. There he noticed a saddle and bridle but not a horse. Probably with the men who'd left their weapons. He dragged the body further down the rocks to find an easier place to bury it. Rye did the only thing he could do for the man. He could have been a trapper whose luck had run out. Any way he looked at it, this man's misfortune saved Blanche and Rye.

***

While Rye took care of the horses, Blanche checked out the inside of the cabin. She found plenty of food that would help them through the winter. Someone had left the food. She didn't care. The cabin would save their lives.

Rye walked in a few moments later, sweating profusely.

"You have to get out of those clothes, or you could catch pneumonia. Here, wrap yourself in this blanket."

Rye hesitated, but Blanche meant business. He stripped down, and she wrapped the blanket around him. She had already started the fire, so the inside had been warming up.

"There's plenty of food here, enough to last throughout the winter. That man saved our lives, Rye."

***

He lay down on the bed and fell asleep. She stared at him and covered him with the Indian blanket to keep her warrior warm. A true warrior. Too bad, he had to die.

Blanche looked around the cabin some more. She had already found the food but wanted to see what else the cabin held. She'd found rifles and boxes of cartridges—way too many for one man. She suspected this cabin was where Duncan and Lily stashed the guns that the Indians had purchased.

She opened a door. Crates of alcohol. Guns and alcohol for Indians. Blanche smiled. They would come soon.

Blanche ambled out the front of the cabin to watch it snow. Five Indians stared at her from a few yards away. She calmly walked into the cabin. Shaking, she hurried over and shook Rye. "We have problems, Rye."

Rye sat up quickly.

"Indians out front."

"Grab the rifle and make sure it's loaded."

Rye went outside. First, he talked to them in English. They just stared at him. He then talked to them in Sioux. They seemed to understand. One rode up and spoke back.

"We are Crow but know Sioux language. How do you know it?"

"Fought Sioux in Minnesota."

"You survived?"

"Yes, tough but we did."

"We kill many Sioux and they kill many of us. Sioux come through here also as do Blackfeet, Arapaho, Cheyenne, and Shoshone."

The Crow turned to leave. The leader turned back and

stared at Rye. He then turned his horse and joined the rest of them. Rye would remember his face.

Blanche walked out and put her arms around Rye. "I didn't know you could speak Sioux."

"I didn't either."

"Well, it is a good thing you do. You saved us once again today."

"No, this time you did, Blanche Park. Thank you."

She glanced at him not sure what to say. Again, he had shown his compassion.

He put his arms around her. She actually snuggled into him but had no idea why. The two stood outside for a moment, enjoying the snow. Finally, Blanche shivered so they walked into the cabin.

"Rye?"

"Yes?"

'I think this cabin belongs to Butler Lily."

"Why do you say that?"

"There's a back room full of rifles, ammunition, and whiskey."

"Lily won't come here, but I do believe Marcus Duncan will show up here sooner or later. That means we can't stay."

"Are you sure? It is shelter, and the snow will slow him down."

Rye turned Blanche toward him and stared into her eyes. "Believe me, he will come. When he comes it won't be just the men you saw with him. There will be more."

"What do you mean?"

"It all makes sense. Lily is not the mastermind of all this; Marcus Duncan is. Or maybe someone else whom Duncan is afraid of."

"Why are you so afraid of him?"

Rye sat down and stared at the floor. Blanche got down on her knees and took his hand, gazing up at him. "Please tell me what has you so spooked. What is it about Duncan?"

He let out a breath. "Marcus Duncan and I fought

together during the war. I led a group of guerrillas who went behind enemy lines to disrupt the Union forces. The group consisted of two dozen men all ruthless and deadly, lethal in every form of killing men.

Rye went on. "After a while going in and out of enemy lines started to take its toll. If captured, we'd have a swift death with the noose. Marcus and I are two of a dozen or so who are left. The men alive joined Marcus Duncan. I went my own way until Murfreesboro."

Both turned as the door burst open, and there stood Marcus Duncan. Blanche quickly moved behind Rye.

"Well, Rye. We meet once more."

Others followed him into the cabin, including two Indians. The two started speaking in their language, eyes as wide as could be.

Duncan turned to listen to what they had to say. He turned back around. "My, my, Rye. Everyone wants a piece of your hide. What did you do to rile up the Sioux so bad?"

Rye didn't say anything.

"No matter, they'll just have to wait in line." Duncan spoke to the Indians and they left the cabin. "Sioux are much different than Crow. Crow will battle the Sioux, while Sioux enjoy killing everyone including Whites."

"And they haven't butchered you yet, Duncan?"

"No, I provide them with guns and whiskey, something they seem to enjoy. They can become awful wicked and mean when they have too much to drink. When they're not drinking, they're lethal. Kind of like you and me during the war."

"You went too far, Marcus."

Marcus backhanded Rye across the mouth, causing Blanche to jump back. "Don't worry, missy. No harm will come to your man...at least not yet." He turned back to Rye. "Why did you leave? I would have followed you to hell and back."

The door opened once more, and in came the two

Indians with white hostages. Seeing Rye, Isabelle ran to him. The others followed right after.

"They killed everyone on the wagon train," Christina said defiantly, pointing at Marcus Duncan.

Another group came in.

"What the hell is this all about, Duncan?" Price Davis asked. Libbie and Butler Lily followed him on his heels.

Duncan spoke to the Sioux in their tongue. "You survived the Sioux slaughter. Of course, I told them to keep you alive." He turned back and spoke to them, motioning them to the room. A few moments later, they came back with a keg of whiskey.

The two Indians downed the whiskey in a few gulps. They eyed Libbie and Christina.

"Call them off, Duncan, or they will die tonight."

The tone of Rye's voice made Duncan spin to face him. It stopped him from saying another word. It didn't stop the Sioux. They came after Christina. Rye pushed her to the side and met them head-on. One gashed him with his knife, but Rye snapped the Indian's neck and slammed the knife into the other warrior, killing him instantly.

A clap of hands. "That is the Captain Rye Tyler I know. Get the Sioux out of here, Bitter."

Bitter called for help, and they dragged the two Indians out. "Oh, Rye, to be fair, the Shoshone are coming after you. I saw what happened out there. So that makes the Confederacy, the Sioux, and now the Shoshone." He looked at Blanche. "It's not too late for you to switch to the winning side."

"I think not." She went over to tend to Rye's arm.

Marcus laughed, then he quickly turned mean. "Remember I may last longer than him."

Again, Blanche said, "I think not."

Duncan glared at Rye and said nothing else. Samuel leaned against the wall quietly looking on.

Marcus spoke up again, "Tell me, Rye, what did you do

to piss the Sioux off, so that they are to kill you on sight?'

Bitter came back in. "The snow is coming down heavier and the wind is blowing stronger."

"Guess we're stuck here for some time. These blizzards can last days."

Mina had come in with a couple of Sioux warriors. She spoke to the two. Marcus whipped around.

"I see you know each other. This should be quite interesting."

He glanced at Blanche. "Ma'am, would you mind joining your sister in cooking up some grub for everyone here?"

Blanche knew what she wanted to say, but for everyone's sake, she smiled sweetly. "Yes, I will help my sister."

"Thank you."

"You're welcome."

"I'll help also," Christina spoke up.

Once the three women were in the kitchen, Blanche brought Christina toward her. "Are you okay?"

"Yes, I am. Now that Rye is here."

Libbie peered at Christina. "You don't know what is about to happen."

"Shut up, Libbie," Blanche whispered.

Christina looked at the both of them. Two sisters who didn't see the same thing. She would have to tell Rye.

"Don't give up. As long as Rye is still alive, we have a chance," Blanche said.

"You think a lot of him, don't you," Christina said.

"Yes, I do. He has been through hell."

"Do you love him?" Christina asked. Libbie stopped, spun around, and studied her.

Blanche ignored the question, although she started to have feelings for him. She turned to Libbie. Libbie glared at her. "Why would it matter to you? As far as you're concerned, you and I are done."

Christina said, "Libbie, something—"

Libbie shook her head to stop Christina.

***

Marcus Duncan walked in. Blanche left with a platter of food. Christina joined Blanche with another tray. Libbie hung back.

"You're right, Marcus. Blanche can be used as leverage. She loves the man."

"I could tell. She's the only person who will persuade him to do what we need him to. Good job, Libbie."

He pulled her to him and tried to kiss her. "I knew I could count on you." She pushed him away.

After he turned around, Libbie wiped her lips.

Blanche served Rye and the kids first, and then the others. Isabelle remained glued to Rye's side.

After the men were fed, Duncan opened up once more. He directed his conversation to Butler Lily and the Davis family. "Why did you leave?"

Neither spoke. One of the Sioux scouts started talking. Marcus listened to every word he had to say. Marcus turned to Lily and Davis. "It seems you ran out on us."

"You're right," Lily said, his voice weak.

Libbie turned to him., "What are you going to do with them?"

Rye shook his head. "You might as well kill them all, Marcus."

Marcus Duncan broke into a full roar. "You would like that, wouldn't you, Captain Tyler?"

"It would whittle the odds down enough."

"That it would. The problem is either the Shoshone or the Sioux will be there to make sure that you die a nice and slow death."

Nobody said anything for a moment.

"What happened to you, Marcus?"

Marcus studied Rye. "You."

"Why do you say that?" Libbie asked.

Blanche moved closer to Rye, putting her hand on his shoulder.

Marcus peered up. "You don't realize how much respect I had for you, Captain Tyler. Our group could have licked the whole Union Army by ourselves." He stopped for a moment. Then he focused on Blanche. "Ma'am, you don't know how lethal Rye is. Did he tell you how he slit a man's throat with a butter knife or killed a man with the perfect throw of a pebble?"

Blanche kept her expression impassive during the conversation. She knew what he had been forced to become. The others didn't realize how dangerous he was.

"I know of at least four times he crawled through enemy lines just to make a kill. No hesitation. He had no remorse. The only man I looked up to. In fact, Captain Tyler is the only person I fear."

He paused. "Then Butler Lily came along, or I should say, Rye's father, and Price Davis. Butler had to try to kill him so Rye would have to hunt him down. That meant I had to chase him down and wound up in Minnesota. Figured I'd get me some of the action and make myself some money. The Sioux and Blackfeet are an added bonus."

Rye's eyes narrowed. "You're playing with Indian fire fraternizing with these tribes out here, Marcus. Sooner or later they'll slit your throat."

"That's a possibility. But it's probably a better chance they'll peel your skin piece-by-piece."

He pivoted and peered at Blanche. "You must be a strong woman for our ole captain to fall for you. I can't ever remember him being with a woman in the three years I fought with him. And not always in the war. While we chased women, he'd calmly and quietly escape to his own little world. I can't even remember him having a drink. But he was lethal."

"I hate to correct you, Duncan."

"What?"

"He still is lethal."

Marcus gave her a wicked smile. "Yes, he is. But we now have you and these three kids. You're what we call leverage. My guess is, especially with you, Blanche Davis, or is it now Blanche Tyler? Rye will do anything I ask of him. And from what I remember about the man, he may even enjoy it."

"Why would you think Rye would even care about me or these kids?"

"If he didn't, why would he haul you along with him?"

Blanche smiled. "Maybe I decided to tag along with him because I wanted to get away from you and everyone else in this room."

Marcus glared at her.

Rye stood. The two Sioux warriors bolted to their feet. Marcus waved his hand to let them know he wasn't going anywhere. He stared out the window. Isabelle had followed Rye. He reached down and picked her up. "This blizzard puts a damper on all the ideas you have for the moment."

Rye looked at the young girl in his arms. "Do you remember the one thing you want most in life?" he asked her.

"Yes."

"Well, little one, your dream will come true from this point on."

Blanche held her breath knowing exactly what he would do. Rye turned around to look at Blanche and winked at her. Libbie also saw it. It confused her. Had he fallen for her?

Marcus jumped up. "Stop him now."

Too late. Rye flew through the window holding Isabelle. He rolled with her and came up sprinting toward the river and into the mountains above.

"Kill him, damn it." Duncan hollered.

Chapter 17

A couple of the Sioux raced out the door with Bitter joining the chase. Bitter fired his weapon in the direction Rye had taken Isabelle. The blinding snow made it difficult for anyone to see.

Marcus screamed, "Find them."

Libbie grabbed Christina and Jeremiah and moved them out of the line of fire. She whispered to Christina, "tell Rye everything is not as it seems. Tell him I'm sorry I called him a traitor and a coward. I didn't mean it."

She peered at her.

"Please tell him," Libbie said. She backed away from the two children once she knew they were safe.

***

Christina looked at her, not sure what to think. Being a young woman, her intuition told her that Libbie cared for Rye. She loved him.

Samuel finally spoke, "Marcus, Rye will not be far away. He can't survive this blizzard. And we sure can't go out there in the blinding snow hunting for him. Think about the final goal."

"I am, damn it. He's the only one that can accomplish the final objective."

No one said anything for a moment. "You're right, Samuel. We can't do anything until the blizzard ends. When it clears up, we'll ride to the cabin."

He went over to the window, then turned back to

Blanche. "You had better hope he survives. If not, I'll have to make a decision. Either take you for myself or turn you over to the Sioux. Either way, you lose."

She didn't say anything. After he walked away, Christina and Jeremiah went to her, and they held each other. Though her eyes were watering, Blanche looked over at Libbie. She was grinning at her.

"Keep the faith, Blanche. He has been through a lot and came out on top," Christina said.

She looked up at her. "You are such a lovely girl and have such a beautiful soul. You're right. He will survive."

The three snuggled into each other and fell asleep in the quiet cabin.

***

In the blowing snow, Rye struggled with Isabelle up the mountain. She had fallen asleep in his arms. Rye tried to keep her as warm as possible until he found a place out of the wind and snow. As luck would have it, the two stumbled into an opening that had shelter.

He scurried into it and set a sleeping Isabelle down on the ground. Rye felt around for something to start a fire. A few moments later, he had one going and warmed his hands. He carried Isabelle close to the fire. She woke up and smiled at him.

"I knew you would protect me." She snuggled back into his chest and fell back to sleep. Rye gazed at the young girl. He would always protect her. He leaned back against the rocks and fell asleep himself. The blizzard roared throughout the evening and into the next day.

Both woke up at the sound of horses, then voices. The blizzard had stopped. Rye shifted his eyes toward the sounds. A horse whinnied and Samuel glanced in their direction. Rye squeezed himself against the wall.

Samuel scanned the area. "There is nothing here." He remained for a moment. The other voice asked the question, "what is so damn special about this man? We should have

127

just killed him and taken the women for our own."

"Marcus wants him for a mission. He'll hold Blanche hostage until he completes it."

"What does he want?"

"He wants him to go north into Blackfeet country and help form an alliance with the tribe."

"I don't know about you, but I'm getting out of this weather and heading toward the cabin. Are you coming?" Samuel asked him.

"Yes, I will be along in a minute."

***

Something had spooked Samuel. He knew Tyler would kill him if he stayed here. Samuel didn't want to face the man alone, even though Rye didn't have a gun.

The other man lingered. A mistake. His eyes widened when he saw Rye Tyler staring at him and pleaded for his life. Rye snapped his neck and took his guns. The horse bolted before he could reach it. No matter, Rye got what he wanted—the guns.

Samuel caught up with the rest of them. Marcus reined his horse and glanced at Samuel. "What happened to you?"

"I checked out a couple of crevices he may have crawled into."

"Well?"

"Nothing," Samuel said. Both peered at Blanche who had stopped to listen.

***

Blanche spurred her horse to catch up with Christina and Jeremiah. "I'm sorry for what has happened to you and the wagon train," she said to them.

"We've been through this just like you have."

"Hang in there a little longer."

"Jeremiah and I have not given up hope. Rye is alive and will find us."

All stopped and turned at the commotion behind them. Rye's horse, the Black, had bucked the person on it off. He tried to get the horse back with no luck.

"Quit your damn fooling around," Duncan hollered. The man inched toward the horse. The horse backed up. A couple of others tried to harness the horse. No luck. The Black cantered toward Blanche and stopped.

"What the hell is this?' Duncan asked.

Blanche didn't say anything.

"Damn, Blanche, every man here has wanted you and now a stupid Black horse runs to you. Shoot the damn horse."

Blanche whispered to the horse, and he galloped away from them toward the rocks and out of sight. Everyone gaped at the horse. They'd not seen anything like it.

Blanche stared at Libbie and Marcus. She turned her horse and they moved on. The horses finally stopped in front of a large, beautiful cabin in the mountains. Blanche gazed at the structure.

"Okay here is where we stop," Marcus Duncan said.

Samuel took Blanche by the arm after they reached the cabin. "I will do what I can to help you get through this, but I'll need your help."

She jerked her arm away from him. "You're helping to kill the man I love, and you are asking me to help you? Go to hell!"

"If you wish," he said. He shoved her toward a back bedroom. Other men dragged Christina and Jeremiah to the same room, pushed them in, and locked the door.

"What are we going to do?" Jeremiah asked.

"We will get out of this. I've seen Rye come up with ways to survive. And he will do it once more."

They all fell silent and held each other. The door opened an hour later, and Samuel stepped in. "My father has asked for you."

"Why should I care?"

"Blanche, you are promised to Marcus. He'll have you anyway he can. As for the children, the Indians will brutalize

Christina, including my father."

"What?"

"Yes. They are that mad. You can continue resisting, but believe me it will do you no good. You and those kids are vulnerable. And if you believe Tyler is going to show up, there's a good possibility he'll either freeze to death out there or the Sioux will take care of him."

Blanche pressed her lips together.

"If I leave here and Marcus comes back for you, well, it won't end well for the two kids. Make no mistake, what I said earlier will occur if he returns."

Blanche stood. "You are all evil."

Samuel laughed.

"What's so funny?" Blanche asked.

"You say I'm evil. You don't know Rye Tyler. He's the reason why we're all like this. You have married the demon's son."

"I am not married to anyone," she said, lifting her chin.

"That's even better. Then there's hope for me after all."

Blanche looked toward the kids. "I will be back," she said.

Samuel stood by the door waiting for her. Blanche walked past him down the hallway. A light shone ahead; she headed toward it with Samuel behind her. For some reason, she felt eyes on her the whole time. It made her shudder.

Blanche walked toward the group. Eyes looked toward her. Then a voice spoke up. "So you're the woman whom Tyler fell for?"

"They are not married, Papa," Samuel said.

Blanche turned. An old man sat in a chair. She kept quiet.

"I can see why my son wanted to take you." He turned to Marcus Duncan, standing near Libbie. "It seems like you had to settle for second fiddle with her sister."

Blanche gave her sister a rueful smile. Libbie remained silent.

"Come over here, girl."

Blanche didn't move.

"If I have to tell you again, it will be much worse."

She slowly walked over to him.

"Sit on my lap."

Blanche hesitated but did as he asked. Once on his lap, he started fidgeting with her hair. "My, you are a beautiful woman."

He reached down the front of her shirt and touched her left breast. Blanche squirmed. He massaged it for a second, and she tried to squirm away from him. He stood up and grabbed her around the throat until she struggled to breathe. "Let me tell you something, woman. Rye Tyler's head will end up on a Sioux lance. Before it does, they will torture him beyond human capabilities. And your eyes will see it all."

He let her go, and Blanche grabbed her throat. The old man said, "I know you've thought that you'd have to bury him. It will come true."

She gasped and crossed her arms. How did this guy know?

"Take her away."

The man called Bitter grabbed her roughly by her arm and pushed her back toward the bedroom. He shoved her into the room.

Christina and Jeremiah ran to her. "Are you okay?"

"Yes, I'm fine. We have to figure a way out of here quickly." She held them tight. "We'd better get some sleep."

***

Christina stirred and looked at the Blanche. "Did you get any sleep?"

"No, I couldn't."

"What happened last night that spooked you so bad?"

"It is better if I don't tell you."

"Horrible?"

Christina put her arms around Blanche.

Blanche shook her head. "It is strange because I hated

131

the man before I even knew him. But when he found me in the marshes in Minnesota, my heart just fluttered, and I knew right then there'd be no else in my life. I knew it at ten. Now at twenty-one, it is there once more."

"Good for you, Blanche."

She turned to Christina.

"You are a pretty woman also, Christina."

"You are beautiful. Rye is fortunate to have you."

She turned away. "I don't know if he wants me. I think he prefers my sister." She looked at Jeremiah, who had just woken up. "All hell is going to break loose, and my family doesn't know what is about to hit them. Oh, yeah, Rye will go into Blackfeet country and do what needs to be done to protect us. My guess is the Blackfeet will rein down on us all. There will be no survivors. Rye might not even be able to stop what they do to all of you here."

The three looked at each other terrified.

***

Rye had carried Isabelle for a couple of miles when he stopped to take a break and put her down.

"How are you doing, Isabelle?"

"I'm okay. Do you think Christina and Jeremiah are okay?"

"I sure hope so."

Rye prepared to take another step when war-painted, grotesque-looking Indians surrounded them. He had seen them earlier. Isabelle screamed and jumped into his arms. The Indians didn't move. These had to be members of the Cheyenne Dog Soldiers.

The Dog Soldier and Reb stared at each other. Rye couldn't figure their identity out until one of the Dog Soldiers jumped off his horse and came over to him. He offered water. Rye started to take it, but he slapped his hands away. The Indian handed the water to Isabelle.

Rye knew that many Indian tribes had respect for children. Isabelle had saved his life for the time being. She took a drink and started to hand it to Rye. The Indian snatched it out of her hands. He held his hands out for her to come. Isabelle snuggled into Rye, and he held her tight.

One of the group said something that stopped the warrior. He climbed back on his horse. The conversation amongst the group became heated. Finally, the chief rode his horse up to Rye.

"I will let you live for now. If we see you once more, your death will be slow and painful." He waved his hand and the warriors disappeared like the wind. Rye looked after them. The odds seemed against them.

"We will find your brother and sister."

"What about Libbie?"

Rye stared at the young girl. "Don't you mean Blanche?"

"I'm only ten, but I'm old enough to know you don't care for Blanche."

Rye ruffled her hair. "Smart little ten-year-old. I'll have to listen to you more often. But in this case, you are wrong. I think Libbie loves another."

"Please, don't ever leave me, but if you must, always come back for me."

"I made you that promise when we jumped out of the window together." He whisked her up in his arms and headed for the cabin.

Chapter 18

Blanche had been looking out the window when the door opened. In stepped Marcus Duncan and Libbie.

"Would you like to join us for breakfast?" Marcus asked.

Blanche glared at him but said politely," we would be glad to."

The three of them walked down the hall with Marcus and Libbie. His mother and father and Samuel, along with a couple of people Blanche had never met sat at the table. Her father, along with Butler Lily, had joined them.

The head of the household glanced up. "Any word on the missing member?"

One of the men Blanche did not know answered, "No sign of him. We've seen Sioux signs."

The man slammed his fist. "Find him now before he's out of our sights forever."

"He will come here," Marcus said.

"And why would he do that?"

"Because she is here."

"She's just a woman. He can find them on any street corner."

Blanche stared at him.

"There is one even more special, father." Blanche looked at their father with narrowed eyes. "You actually believe that Rye Tyler gives a damn about any of us in this room?"

The father stood. "I believe he does, madam. If he's anything like your tiger cat, he'll be coming through these doors at any moment."

"And you would be right," Rye said, who had quietly slipped through the door. "Don't try it, Marcus. I would just as soon shoot you here and now."

Blanche, Christina, and Jeremiah moved away from the table. "Everyone slowly takes their guns out and places them in front of them on the table."

"Do you think—" The old woman didn't finish. Rye fired a shot right between her eyes. He strode to Duncan and whispered in his ear, "That is for what you did to Blanche's father."

Libbie looked at Rye, then stepped back out of the way.

"Jeremiah, gather all the guns. Take one for yourself and don't hesitate to shoot anyone that moves. Oh, by the way, each of you take off your boots, as well."

"I'll be damned." Again, Rye turned and shot the person point blank between the eyes.

The rest quickly did as he said without a word.

Rye quickly tied their hands together. He came to Samuel. "I gave you an opportunity to do the right thing. Now, it's too late."

Just as Rye started to leave the room, Marcus said, "This isn't over by any means. You will pay for my mother's death and more."

He pointed his pistol at Marcus and hesitated. Blanche touched his arm. He saw her pleading eyes. "Yes, it is, Marcus. I'm going where you can't find me. I ran into Cheyenne Dog Soldiers. They may have mentioned to me that a white man isn't welcome in their country."

Rye strode toward the door but stopped and gazed at Libbie. His eyes met hers. He could have sworn her lips said, "be careful." He then glared at the old man sitting in the chair. Hatred filled his eyes. The old man's scowl darted from Libbie Davis to Rye. He knew.

"Where the hell are the guards?" Marcus yelled as Rye left. Isabelle did her best to hold onto the horses when they walked out. Christina, Isabelle, and Jeremiah held each other crying. Blanche put her arms around Rye's shoulders and kissed him passionately.

"We have to get out of here. I've bought us some time, but they will be coming after us. I'm hoping you two youngsters can handle horses, because where we're going, the terrain will be rough."

"Point out the direction," Jeremiah said.

Rye smiled and climbed on his horse. He headed north.

Blanche caught up with him. "Isn't that Blackfeet country?"

"Yep," he said.

"But?"

"Don't worry. We will need some allies. Maybe the Blackfeet will be our allies for a bit. Besides, we have an ace."

"Who?"

"This little one here," he said, ruffling up her hair. She smiled up at him. "I'll explain later. Now we need to cover as much distance as we can."

***

Back in the cabin, Marcus Duncan threw things around the room. "Let's go, men. We're going after them. This is going to end."

His father didn't say anything at first. Finally, he spoke up. "Go avenge the murder of your mother." The old man did not move. He continued to watch Libbie. She noticed his interest and tried to go out the door. "No, young lady. You and I will have a chat."

"I don't have anything to say to you."

"Well, missy, I have some questions for you. You know Rye Tyler?"

"Everyone knows Mister Tyler."

"I mean, you are the ten-year-old who has searched for the man over the years."

"If I am, it sure isn't any of your business."

The old man laughed.

"I believe you are the person I need to keep close to me. Your sister means nothing to him. What to do with you?"

Both spun around as the door burst open. Libbie jumped back as her older brother stormed in with several Blackfoot warriors.

"Well, Mister Davis," the old man said. "How have you been? I see you brought some friends with you."

"As you asked. They will meet with you and Rye."

"That is good. We'll just have to find him now."

"That could be difficult."

The old man glanced at Libbie. "I don't think so. We keep your sister near, and he will show up."

Wade looked at Libbie. "I look forward to spending more time with you, sis."

Libbie didn't say anything. Wade turned to the old man. "Are you ready to get away from here?"

"Yes. It is time for us to leave. Your sister and I have much to discuss."

***

Rye led the way away from the cabin heading north. From his calculations, it would take at least a week to reach Blackfeet territory. He had no plans of actually going into Blackfeet Territory, hoping the men Marcus Duncan would send to chase him down would think that. They would escape over the mountains and head south.

Blanche rode up next to him. Christina had taken her little sister to ride with her. "Are you okay?"

"Yes, just thinking about how to get out of this mess."

"Why did you kill that woman? Their mother."

"All I could think of was Marcus slicing your father's ear."

"But you killed her in such a cold-blooded way"

Rye stopped his horse. "Yes, I did. If anyone would have opened their mouth, I would have shot them dead as well." He looked at her. "I told Samuel I would come for you. Once

I take you to safety, I will finish this once and for all. You should have let me kill him." He rode on.

Blanche studied Rye. She had never seen him like this before. Of course, no one really knew him. The man was locked in a zone that she had only heard about but had never seen until now. Bent on revenge, he would stop at nothing.

**

Rye reined in his horse. Blanche followed suit, as did the kids behind them. He looked at the Cheyenne Dog Soldiers who sat on their horses on the peak ahead of them. Had they seen the small group? They must have. He stood up on his stirrups and turned to look around. Dust billowed from what must have been Marcus Duncan.

"Over here quickly," he motioned to Blanche and the kids. They followed him up a tight trail into an area where they would be hidden. He jumped off his horse and motioned for the others to do the same. "We have to make sure the horses don't let the others know we're here. Keep them quiet."

They complied. Ten minutes later a string of horses rode through the canyon. Duncan's men. Rye counted at least twenty or more of them. He didn't know the number of Cheyenne Dog Soldiers. It didn't matter because once the men moved into the open, the Dog Soldiers would strike. Nothing Rye could do about it.

They looked on as the fighting began. The Dog Soldiers swept down upon them. Duncan's men didn't have a chance.

"We have to take these children to safety." he said.

"Are you okay?" Blanche said.

"Yes, I am. Now let's move out of here." Rye guided his horse through the trail. Blanche followed and Jeremiah brought up the rear. At times they could barely squeeze through the pass. The gunfire continued. Then silence.

Rye stopped suddenly.

"Here, hold the horses, Blanche."

Before she could answer, he scrambled up to a better

vantage point. The Dog Soldiers were climbing through the pass. He quickly moved back to the horses.

"What is it?"

"The Indians are coming. I thought they'd seen us but hoped they would be more intent on Duncan's men and leave us alone."

Blanche stood speechless. Then she roused herself to action and hopped on her horse as the others did.

Rye rode back and took Isabelle from Christina. "It's going to be tough going, and we'll be moving fast. I won't kid you. The odds aren't very good." He headed his horse toward the pass. The others struggled to keep up with him, but they did the best they could. They had ridden hard for fifteen minutes when Rye called a halt. From the top of the peak, he could see everything in all directions. "You all hide here. They will not see you. I'll lead them away."

The Dog Soldiers were gaining on them. Rye spotted an open area on the other side of the mountain. It would take them a few moments to reach it, and hopefully he would be across. With no other choice, he started down the other side. Just as they reached the bottom, the Dog Soldiers came screaming over the mountain and raced down the trail.

Rye went into a gallop and then a run. He turned his horse toward the Cheyenne. As soon as the first soldier reached the bottom of the mountain, he nailed him with his rifle, then a second and a third.

At that point the Cheyenne came riding down in droves. He turned his horse around and spurred him. One hit Rye's horse, knocking him down. The Dog Soldiers circled him. Rye passed out.

***

Christina ran down the mountain. The Dog Soldiers turned and watched the young woman run down the mountain toward the man they had just shot. She pleaded with the Indians to let her take care of him.

They moved back.

Blood poured out of his chest. She knew enough about wounds to realize that he had lost too much blood. She ripped layers off her skirt and pressed the pieces down on his chest to stop the bleeding.

Tears streamed down her face. Isabelle, who had followed her, tugged on Christina's coat, then looked up. The Cheyenne Dog Soldiers sat on their horses in a circle around the three. Christina stood and stared at the painted faces of angry men, then dropped to the ground, pulled Isabelle toward her, and held her little sister tightly.

Chapter 19

Christina looked up at the grotesque faces of the Cheyenne once more. They had not moved. They just stared at her and her sister.

"Isabelle, help me get Rye on the horse."

The two tried to lift him onto the horse but couldn't. The Black first went down on his front knees and then his hind quarter to allow them to place Rye on the saddle. The Dog Soldiers shook their heads and muttered at what the Black had just done.

Isabelle and Christina lifted him onto the horse. Christina tied his hands onto the saddle horn to keep him from falling off. "Hold onto him the best you can, Isabelle."

"I won't let him go, big sister."

Christina smiled at her little sister. She would do anything for this man. She took the reins and walked toward the circle of Dog Soldiers, then stopped at the chief's horse. "Please move your horse," she asked, not knowing or even caring if he understood a word she said.

The chief studied her for a moment and then moved aside. Christina walked toward the mountain pass that they had come from.

Christina could feel the Dog Soldiers' stares on her back but continued to walk, tears flowing down her cheeks. If dead, Christina would bring Rye to a place that he would die in peace.

She reached the pass and struggled to climb it. Isabelle

jumped off and helped her. It took at least fifteen minutes of hard work, but the two made it to the top. When they reached the crest, Christina turned and looked down at the Dog Soldiers. They had not moved. Jeremiah and Blanche joined the two young ladies.

Christina glared at the woman. "If you truly love this man as you say, you would have done what you could to save him."

"Who do you think you are?"

Christina didn't say a word to the woman. Silently, they descended the other side. Another hour passed before they made it to the spot where the Dog Soldiers had attacked and killed all of those who had earlier tried to kill Rye and the others. They stopped and looked at the carnage. None were alive, and all had been scalped. Lily, Samuel, and Price Davis, along with Rye's brothers were all dead. No Libbie. Thank God, Christina thought to herself.

Nobody felt any remorse. They deserved everything they received. The sun had set when they returned to the cabin.

Blanche stopped the horse on the porch and collapsed.

Christina opened the door and then went to drag Rye into the house. "Please help me, Jeremiah?"

The two struggled to carry him into the house and onto one of the beds. Blanche worked on him. Rye's breathing continued to be sporadic.

Christina stared at Blanche. "We are alive. We have to continue living. That is what he would have wanted." She couldn't figure out where the bullet went, so she turned him over and saw it had gone through. Christina broke down in tears. "You will make it, Rye Tyler. Someone else needs you." Christina peered at Isabelle, who had fallen asleep beside Rye. She turned and stroked his hair. "Wake up, Rye. I need you. We need you." With that she fell asleep lying on his chest.

The next morning Isabelle woke up. She jumped onto the bed with Rye.

"Careful, Isabelle. He is not doing well," Christina said, who checked on him.

"I'm sorry. I have always wanted to do that."

She smiled. "Maybe you should wait until he is healed. I'm sure he'll enjoy you doing that."

Isabelle smiled back and started to head out of the bedroom. She stopped and looked at her. "Rye is my father. I love him." The girl bounded out of the room to Blanche and Jeremiah. Tears flowed from Christina's eyes. She prayed that Rye would come back to them, then scrubbed away her tears and wiped his fevered brow.

Over the next few days, Blanche and Christina did what they could for Rye. Isabelle stayed with him unless she had to eat.

The young girl came running inside. "Hurry Christina, some men are out front."

Christina stepped onto the front porch. Isabelle huddled behind her. Jeremiah pointed a rife at a dozen men.

"My, my. A couple of beautiful women. Where are the menfolk?

"My husband will be back soon," Blanche said, who had stepped out with them. "Jeremiah is awful handy with the rifle."

"And who might that be? I understand this is the Duncan place."

Nobody said anything for a moment. Christina noticed Blanche's lifted chin. Did she know them?

"I don't believe any of you. My guess is—it's just the three of you, and you are waiting for the Duncans to come back from a raid. The twelve of us will help ourselves to your women's company until they return."

"I doubt it."

Blanche whipped around. "Honey, it is you. Where have you been?" She ran to his side.

The leader gaped at him. A man whispered next to him. "Watch it. That's Rye Tyler."

He backed up a few steps. "We'd best move along. I'm sorry to disturb you." They rode away.

Blanche reached up and kissed Rye on the lips.

"Hold it. Are you trying to kiss me or kill me?"

Isabelle ran up to him and jumped into his arms. "I knew you would survive."

"No, little one, you saved us." He turned to Christina. "Thank you, Christina. "He took her hand. "Thanks for dragging me up and down those damn mountains."

"What? How did you know?"

"I saw your shining face before I passed out." He looked around the cabin. "That is the only way I could have gotten back here. The Dog Soldiers wouldn't have hauled me back. But it is curious how you managed it."

"I'll tell you. But first, I'll get you something to eat."

"I am hungry."

Blanche started to walk away, then stopped and looked at him. "How can you be alive?"

Rye grinned. "Blanche, you'll find out I'm hard to kill. You'll just have to try harder."

Chapter 20

Rye savored each bite. He listened as Christina explained what happened with the Cheyenne. "I've heard stories about Indians respecting bravery. My guess—they were amazed at what you did to save me, Christina."

"We weren't about to let anything happen to you," Isabelle added. "You've saved our lives more than once."

Rye smiled, reaching over to ruffle her hair.

"The question is—what are we going to do now?" Blanche asked.

"I don't think anyone would mind if we spent the winter here in this cabin," Rye said.

***

Rye and Isabelle stopped by the frozen creek within sight of the cabin. They sat down on a log and enjoyed the view.

"You know, whoever built the cabin did a good job of positioning it for protection," Rye said. He glanced down at his companion when she didn't answer.

"Do you think my mother and father are up in heaven?" Isabelle asked. Tears streamed down her face. Rye took her hand, pulled her close, and held her in his arms.

"Yes I believe they are in heaven and are looking down on you."

Isabelle looked at him. "I don't want them to be in heaven when I go there."

Rye didn't know what to think or how to respond.

Isabelle peered up at Rye and then pointed.

Rye stifled a gasp at the Dog Soldier standing like a statue nearby. Other warriors came out of the trees. Rye had no choice but to wait and see what would happen.

The chief rode his horse slowly toward the two. The others stayed. He stopped in front of him and stared for a moment, then turned to his warriors and spoke in their native tongue. "You have survived," the chief said in perfect English to Rye.

"Where did you learn my tongue?"

"We have captured many whites. They talk before they die."

Rye said nothing. The chief looked at the little girl and smiled. "She is a brave girl. The other woman is brave."

"What do you mean?"

"She dragged you up over the mountain to safety."

"Did any survive the fight?"

"No. They all died. Several killed themselves rather than face honor. I believe you would have faced honor rather than die a coward. Many got away."

Rye reflected on the chief's words, then said, "All I have ever wanted was to live in peace. Thank you for that opportunity."

"Don't thank me. You have earned it. Remember, White man. I said the next time we catch you, your death would be horrible. The Dog Soldiers have asked that your life be spared. And those of this little girl and the brave woman who came amidst our Dog Soldiers. It is very rare, but it will be granted."

He turned to ride away, then stopped and turned around. "Be wary. There are more Whites in these mountains."

The chief rode away. As soon as he did, the Dog Soldiers followed him. Rye counted at least a dozen Dog Soldiers dressed in war paint.

"I guess we'd better head back to the cabin. Remember, don't say anything to anybody. They don't need to worry about our guardians."

The two stepped inside. Rye smoothed Isabelle's hair. "Why don't you go choose one of the rooms for yourself?"

Rye took Blanche by the hand and walked to the porch with her.

"What is it?" she asked.

"Much of what Marcus and Butler said is true. I am a brutal murderer. That will never change. But you know that." He didn't stop to wait for her reaction but continued. "You saw some of that darkness with Marcus's mother." He looked at Blanche. "We know what each has to do, and we're stuck with each other for the time being. Sooner or later it will end."

***

Blanche glared at the man. "You have no clue what you are into, Rye."

Both turned when the door opened, and Isabelle came out and grabbed Rye's hand. "I'm tired and I'm hungry."

Blanche smiled. "We'll get something, sweetheart."

Isabelle looked at her. "Please, don't call me that."

Blanche's eyes flinched, she walked in the cabin, and whipped together a meal.

***

While eating, Isabelle rubbed her sleepy eyes. Christina and Jeremiah yawned.

When Isabelle finished eating, Christina stood. "Come on, Isabelle, I'll tuck you into bed."

She nodded and took Christina's hand, but then spun around, ran, and jumped into Rye's arms. "Good night, Dad. I love you."

Rye glanced at Christina. He turned back to Isabelle. "Good night, little one. I love you too. You are safe now."

Isabelle jumped out of his arms and ran back to Christina. "I want the bedroom near Rye. I know I'll be safe then."

"It's a deal," Christina said. She stayed in the bedroom

147

with the young girl. Her little sister was scared, so she held her tight.

"Please don't let Rye leave us. I feel safe around him."

"Isabelle, I don't know what will happen with any of us. One thing I promise—even if Jeremiah and I wind up somewhere else, I will make sure Rye protects you."

"Thank you, big sister. You have always been my mother. I know you do it because I'm your sister, but someday someone will take your place. Then I won't be a burden."

"Sweetie, you have never been a burden. You are my little sister, and I will always take care of you."

Isabelle rolled over and within a few minutes fell asleep. Christina made sure she fell asleep before she covered her up, then went out to find her brother.

Rye stared at Jeremiah and Christina. "This has been a lot for all of you. I promise I'll do my best to help you guys have a normal life."

Jeremiah gave him a rare hug. "I'm going to find a room in back to sleep in. Good night."

Christina frowned at Rye. "I'm worried something will happen to you."

"What?"

"Libbie whispered to me to tell you that everything isn't what it seems. Please be careful. From a woman's perspective, be wary of Blanche. Libbie also said she didn't mean what she said that you are a coward or traitor."

He smiled at her. "I know she didn't. I'll remember what you said. Good night and thank you." He kissed her on the cheek. She smiled and walked down the hallway.

***

Rye turned toward the front door of the cabin and walked out. Blanche glanced up as he came out.

"Don't waste your time, Rye."

"What are you talking about?"

"You're right. We are stuck with each other. There's no

way I will say anything to you about what is happening. It is better for both of us to survive."

"I see. Keep those three children out of whatever you and your gang are hatching."

Blanche's eyes narrowed. "I can't guarantee that. I can guarantee that your time will come; I just don't know when. I'm going to bed." Blanche slipped into the cabin.

The next morning little Isabelle was sitting on the couch next to Rye, staring at him with glaring little eyes. "Well?"

"Well what?" Rye asked. He stretched and yawned.

"I'm hungry, so since you are my pa now, it would be nice to get something to eat." Her head tilted, and they both laughed. Rye rolled off the couch, picked up Isabelle, and carried the giggling girl into the kitchen.

"Maybe I don't want to be your father."

"You don't have a choice. You're stuck with me," she said smiling at him.

***

Blanche lay in the bed for a moment hearing her giggle. This was how she had envisioned being married and having a child with her true love was like. She finally crawled out of bed and got dressed, the wonderful aroma of bacon wafting in. Within a few minutes, everyone sat around the table eating breakfast.

"What are we going to do today?" Isabelle asked.

"What do you want to do?" Rye asked.

Isabelle thought for a moment. "Can we go exploring?"

Blanche glanced at Rye. "I'll stick around here and do some cleaning and see what we have. There are still a few months of winter left. You want to help me, Christina?"

"Yes," she said.

"Will you be okay?" Rye asked.

"Yes, I will."

"We won't travel too far away. Jeremiah, you want to join us?"

A big grin covered his face. "I sure don't want to be here

with women."

Everyone laughed.

Isabelle climbed down off her chair. "Are you ready?"

"Let's go," Rye said.

***

Isabelle took his hand and led him toward the door. Jeremiah had walked out ahead of them. The three headed toward the river and strolled along the riverbed. Isabelle remained silent for a moment, then said, "It's so beautiful out there."

"Yes, it sure is," he said to her. "What do you think, Jeremiah?"

"No one has ever asked how I felt about anything."

Rye looked at the young man. He felt sorry for him. "It is nice to have a man around to help me out."

Jeremiah smiled.

Isabelle took Rye's hand once more and continued walking, then stopped quickly at the sight of an Indian.

"It's okay. He means no harm," Rye said.

"Is it one of the Indians we saw the other day?"

"Yes, it is," Rye responded.

"Why are they out here?"

"I don't know, but we had better head back to Blanche and Christina." He glanced at Jeremiah. "Take Isabelle back and watch over her."

Jeremiah nodded and walked Isabelle back to the house. Rye followed at a slower pace. When they returned, at least a dozen horses were tied at the front.

"Who are they?"

"I don't know, but we'll be careful."

Rye carried Isabelle to the porch. He set her down and stepped inside with his gun drawn. Jeremiah stayed right behind him. The sergeant from Ridgely and several other Union soldiers sat at the table laughing when the three walked in.

At the sight of Rye, Blanche stood, went over to Rye,

and took his hand. "Look who showed up on our doorstep."

Rye was surprised to see the sergeant from Minnesota all the way here in the mountains. The sergeant sensed it. He stood and came over to shake Rye's hand.

"Good to see you again, Captain."

"How are things going, Sergeant?" Rye said.

"Good. Survived the Minnesota conflict. Now we're into another one in the west." The sergeant peered around. "Can we talk?"

Rye nodded at him. "Isabelle, can you go into your bedroom for a few minutes?"

She did as asked. Blanche continued holding Rye's left hand, but he gently released his other one. "What you have to say can be said in front of Blanche, Christina, and Jeremiah."

"We're up from Fort Laramie on a mission to look for a group of Confederate soldiers."

"The twelve of you?"

"No, we're a group of soldiers scouring throughout the mountains looking for them. We just happened to come upon this cabin, and lo and behold, we found Blanche here."

Rye's eyes narrowed. "You just happened to wind up here in the mountains and found us?"

The sergeant continued as if he hadn't heard Rye. "We want you to guide us up to Montana through the Blackfeet nation."

"What makes you think I can do that?"

"I'm talking to the same man who made it through the whole Sioux nation with that young beauty you have standing next to you."

Rye said nothing at first, then, "Not going to do it,"

"I was hoping you wouldn't be a disagreeable captain. I have orders to arrest you on the spot if you decide not to. I don't want to have to do that."

"And what about Blanche and the three children?"

"I will leave a couple of men here to protect them."

"You will, will you?"

"You can't get away with this. There is nowhere for you to run. Everybody knows you are here. If you take us up north, I have a pardon for you from the U.S. government." He pulled out a piece of paper. "Think about it, Captain. You will be a free man." The sergeant handed him the paper—a pardon signed by the president of the United States.

He looked at Blanche. She nodded to him. "I will do it, but Isabelle will go with us."

The sergeant frowned. "It is going to be tough enough getting us through. What makes you think it will be any easier with her?"

"It won't be. I made a promise to protect her."

The sergeant stared at him.

"That is the way it will be, or you can go ahead and continue sending your hounds after me."

He walked into Isabelle's room.

***

Blanche looked at them. "We have plenty of space if you all would like to bed down inside the cabin tonight. There are some rooms in the back you can use."

"Thank you, ma'am," the sergeant said. She led them to the back to the room she had stayed and the one across the way. She showed them where they could wash up. "Lunch will be ready around noon." Blanche peered down the hall and then turned back to the sergeant. "What are you doing here? This wasn't part of the plan."

"Something is happening. Libbie is missing. Duncan is looking for her. Ben believes that she may be heading this way to find Rye and tell him everything."

"That can't happen."

"I know, Blanche, but she can't be found."

"Damn her," Blanche said. "Why docsn't Bcn just kill her and get it over with?"

"I can't answer that. I just wanted you to know." No one spoke for a few seconds. He looked at her and smiled. "We all have a part to play."

"Enough," she said.

She headed to the kitchen to start lunch. Rye was sitting on the front porch with Isabelle. Blanche stepped out. The soldiers had already come out to take care of their horses. She sat down and took his hand. "Are you okay?"

"Will it ever end?" he asked.

Chapter 21

The motley group sat down for lunch.

"The soup is very tasty," the sergeant remarked.

"Well, thank you, Sergeant," Blanche responded.

While eating, the sergeant asked Rye, "How long do you think it will take for us to reach Montana?"

"I've never been to Montana, so I'm in the same place you are. Quite frankly, Sergeant, you haven't told me anything that gives me a reason to help you out."

"I know you fought for the Confederacy, Captain, but the war will be over soon, and you'll have to make a decision about whether you want to be on the winning team or not."

Rye stood. "What happened to you? You're not the same man I knew in Minnesota."

The sergeant looked at him and didn't say anything.

Rye strode out the door. Isabelle jumped down and ran after him. She caught up to him heading down to the river. Rye stopped, and she took his hand. He smiled at her. *The ole' girl just can't stay away from me.*

She smiled back at him. "I feel safe with you. Those men I don't trust."

"Neither do I."

They had only walked a little further when they heard the first shots that came from near the house.

"Stay here in the bushes," he said. "Don't come out until I come and get you."

She nodded, and Rye raced toward the house. Blanche would have ducked out of the way. He snapped a shot, killing a man on horseback wearing a Confederate uniform. The shooting had ceased, but the other men on horses had disappeared back into the mountains.

He rushed into the house and hollered for Blanche, Christina, and Jeremiah.

The two children yelled back that they were okay.

"I'm okay," Blanche said, stepping out of the bedroom. She ran to him and put her arms around him. He held her tight.

"Where is Isabelle?"

"She is safe."

Rye looked around at the soldiers on the floor. Several had died. Blanche went from soldier to soldier to see whom she could help.

Rye ran outside to grab Isabelle. She hadn't left the spot. He picked her up. As he did, he spied a Cheyenne Dog Soldier sitting on his horse in the tree line who turned and drifted away. Rye looked down at the girl. The Dog Soldier had watched over her. "Everyone is okay. There will be dead soldiers in the house." He carried her quickly back to the cabin and into her room. "Stay here, and you will be safe.'

"I know." She smiled at him.

Christina was working on one of the men. Four had died. He glanced at Blanche who was helping one of the men. The man started crying, then his lifeless eyes stared at the ceiling.

Christina peered up at Rye with a tear in her eye and shook her head. Rye took her hands, pulled her up, and held her tightly.

"Isabelle is in her bedroom. Go on and be with her. I'll bury these men." It took him and Jeremiah most of the afternoon to do it. When finished they sat on the porch with Christina. Blanche stepped out with Isabelle.

"What happened?" Blanche asked.

"I don't know. It is like the Rebs and the Union soldiers

disappeared. How did they know the Union soldiers had been here? What happened to the sergeant and the rest of his men?"

"I saw them slip out after the shooting started."

Rye didn't say anything at first. He stared out toward the river. "They are gone now, Blanche, but they'll be back."

Isabelle spoke up. "Do you think it's okay if we eat?"

"Are you getting hungry?" Rye asked.

Isabelle's eyes brightened. "Yes."

Blanche and Rye smiled at each other

"I guess I'll get something started," Christina said.

Isabelle jumped up and ran into the house with her big sister

After a few minutes, Rye stood and as he did, he noticed a Cheyenne Dog Soldier sitting on his horse. Rye walked toward him. The warrior didn't move. "Thank you for watching over Isabelle."

The Dog Soldier didn't say anything for a moment. He looked at the house and then down at Rye. "Three beautiful women you have."

Rye nodded.

The Dog Soldier spoke once more, "We will watch over your family. No harm will come to them." He started to turn away. "Or you." With that he disappeared into the woods.

Rye turned to Blanche's voice.

"What did the Blackfoot say?"

Rye didn't say anything until he reached her. "No, Cheyenne Dog Soldier. He said they would be watching over all of us. They'd make sure no harm came to you."

"That's nice to know," she said.

Chapter 22

Christina had whipped up a full course meal of beef and potatoes. Isabelle gobbled hers as if she hadn't eaten for some time. Rye enjoyed every bite

"This is very good, Christina. I can tell right now I'm going to enjoy your cooking." He looked at Blanche. "Where did this come from?"

"There is a storage of food down in the basement of the house. They had prepared to hole up here for a while." Blanche started to clear the table.

Christina stopped her. "Isabelle and I can clear the table. Go take a break."

"Thanks," she said, kissing her on the cheek. Blanche walked toward the bedroom.

Christina said to Isabelle, "Well little one, are you ready to help?"

She jumped up, grabbed a dish, and walked toward the kitchen.

Christina smiled and took the other ones. After clearing the dishes, she started running some water. Then she pulled up a chair for Isabelle to stand on. "Here you go, little one. You can help also." Christina gazed at Isabelle. "I love you, little sister. I am so happy that we can do something together."

Isabelle frowned. "Do you think Rye will keep us?"

Christina glanced toward the living room. "Yes, I believe he will do everything he can to protect us." What she didn't tell her was she didn't know if it would be enough.

The two did the dishes in comfortable silence. When finished Christina took her little sister into the bedroom. She closed the door and sat down next to her. "Isabelle, Rye will do everything he can to protect us. But you have to be prepared for what is about to happen."

"What is about to happen?"

"I don't know, little one, but there is just so much going on that is hard to understand. Blanche is having a battle within her, so be careful of her."

"I will, big sister. What about Rye? He would never do anything to hurt us."

"No, Isabelle. He won't. You can trust him with your life."

Isabelle smiled. "Good."

She walked outside and sat down next to Rye. Rye rubbed her hair.

They chatted about nothing and everything. It took a half an hour or so before Isabelle started rubbing her eyes. She slid down on Rye's lap and fell asleep within minutes. Rye picked Isabelle up and tucked her into bed. He kissed her on the forehead and said good night. Isabelle, half-awake, said "I love you, Dad." She fell right to sleep.

Rye went back out, and Christina glanced up at him. She reached into her left breast and pulled out a piece of paper.

"What is that?"

"It is the pardon the sergeant promised you."

"How did you get it?"

"You're not the only one with skills."

Rye grinned at the young woman. "You're growing up quickly, Christina."

"I am eighteen, Rye."

"I know. I mean that you have gone through so much— you all have. You deserve to have a better life. Hopefully that will happen."

"We will. I believe it deep down. I also believe you will

guide us in that direction." She rose and started to walk inside. "Rye, I am just glad that you are here for Isabelle."

"What is that all about?"

"Someday I will tell you. Good night."

Christina walked into the cabin leaving Rye by himself. He sat there gazing out into the mountains.

***

Libbie gazed at him. She had been deciding whether or not to go to Rye. She turned quickly at the noise. Marcus Duncan and her brother, Wade, had come up behind her.

"I figured sooner or later you would make your way back here," Wade said.

She looked toward the cabin. "Please let me go to him."

Marcus laughed. "Your choice, Libbie. You know what happens if you do."

Libbie stared again at the man she had dreamed about for so many years. She rounded her horse back toward the mountains alongside Duncan and her brother.

Indians with grotesque faces surrounded them before she could react. Their rifles pointed at them. No one said a word.

Finally, Wade spoke up, talking to them in English. "Why are you here?"

The six Dog Soldiers said nothing. They stared at Libbie. Wade looked at what caught their attention. "Take her. She means nothing to us," Marcus said.

Libbie glanced at them, her mouth forming a single line. She couldn't believe what she just heard.

One of the Dog Soldiers moved forward a step. "I see you are a coward, turning this woman over to Dog Soldiers. You know what we do with White women. She will be the chief's woman."

"If it means my survival, you can have her," Marcus muttered.

"We should kill you and let her go."

This seemed to scare Marcus. Dog Soldier looked at Wade. He appeared to know him. He turned back to Libbie.

"I believe you would be better suited for the man who lives in this cabin. Man named Rye Tyler."

Libbie felt her heart skip a beat.

Wade grabbed her shoulder. "No, she belongs with us."

The Dog Soldier studied Wade, then turned back to Libbie. "Too bad, young lady. You are strong like the man in the cabin. Not cowardly like these two." With that the Dog Soldiers vanished. Tears ran down her cheeks as she stared at the cabin. She scrubbed her cheeks with a hand and turned to Wade. "He knew you, didn't he?"

"He did. We had hoped to use them to help, but Rye changed that."

"Everything has changed. I think Blanche is way too close to Rye."

Does that bother you, sis?"

"It did before. I have no feeling now."

"Let's go, Libbie."

Libbie hesitated. She desperately wanted to go to Rye.

"Come on. He's in love with Blanche. He doesn't care about you at this point," Wade said. "He has been with her for months now. You think they aren't playing house together?"

Duncan laughed. Libbie glared at the man. She turned her horse and raced away from the cabin. She stopped quickly and turned toward the two. "Rye knows that he's being used."

She rode away. The two followed.

Chapter 23

Rye could see the eyes staring at him from above. He grabbed the little girl and started tickling her. "Are you ever going to let me sleep?"

"No. This will be my routine every day."

"Then I will have to be up before you, won't I?" He stopped and looked at the little girl. "Isabelle, you don't have to wake up early every morning to make sure I'm here. I will always be here. You can count on that. Deal?"

"It's a deal," Isabelle said.

Rye and Isabelle headed into the kitchen and cooked breakfast.

"It smells good. It must be your cooking, Isabelle? I've never smelled bacon that good with Blanche cooking."

Isabelle's grin showed her satisfaction. The three sat down to breakfast. Jeremiah and Christina joined them a few minutes later.

Blanche asked Rye what his plans were for the day.

"Think I'm going to climb on the Black and take a look around."

"Can I go with you?" Isabelle asked.

"Not today, little one. You stay and help Blanche and Christina around the cabin. If you're up to it, Jeremiah, I want you to come along."

A grin spread across his face. "Yes, I will."

Isabelle pouted and folded her arms across her chest but said she'd stay.

After breakfast, Blanche packed Rye and Jeremiah each a lunch of meat and bread to take with him. Isabelle had run into her bedroom and came running back out. She handed Rye a necklace.

"What's this for?"

"To protect you out there. Christina bought it so I wouldn't be afraid. If you put it around your neck, you will never be afraid."

"Thanks, little one. It will protect me." He slipped it around his neck. Rye bent down and kissed her on the forehead. "Don't worry. The Indians will protect us."

Isabelle turned toward Blanche. "Can you take me down to the river?"

"I can do that, Isabelle."

Christina stated she would stay around the house. Rye knew she didn't trust Blanche but for some reason Isabelle did.

Blanche smiled at Isabelle, took her hand, and they headed toward the river.

***

Rye and Jeremiah had traveled north for about an hour when they came to the site of the massacre. The bodies were gone. Rye paused for a moment looking around the area. Nothing seemed out of the ordinary as far as he could tell.

"This tragedy didn't have to happen," Jeremiah said.

"I agree."

He climbed off the Black and slowly walked toward the place where many had died together. Jeremiah stayed with the horses. Rye knelt down at one spot when he saw something glistening. A pendant. He opened it. Inside was a photo of everyone in his family except him. And a picture of a man he had never seen before. He looked older than the rest of the family. Who could it be?

Rye threw it back down on the ground and buried it with his foot. He shuffled around a bit more, searching for anything that would give him an idea of what had happened.

He made his way to the wooded area and found two sets of hoof prints. Two horses had escaped through here before the battle. His guess—Duncan ran out on everyone. He had done it before. The other footprints weren't as deep, meaning Libbie may have been with him. He couldn't imagine what kind of person would bring a woman out on something like this.

Rye returned to his horse, and they followed the trail. They rode into a dense forest and continued traveling into it deeper and deeper. He stopped after about thirty minutes. A noise caught his attention. He drifted toward the sound. Another thirty minutes and Rye and Jeremiah came to an opening. Rye took stock of the area. Ahead a mountain peak. To the right a wall of mountains. To the left a trail.

The two hoofprints went down the trail. They followed the trail for another fifteen minutes. The sound was getting louder, so he pulled out his pistol. The trail became steeper and tighter. Slowly he moved upward. Jeremiah followed close behind.

"Wait here, Jeremiah. Cover my back."

He said he would.

Rye rode to the top of a peak and the trail ended. Looking down he saw a lake. Near it sat at least a dozen wagons in a valley in the middle of the mountains.

He scanned the area but saw nothing except the pink clouds heralding a storm, possibly a blizzard from the north. Rye sighed and slowly traveled down the mountain because there was no trail to speak of.

He rode into the camp. No one made any effort to stop him. When Rye reached the wagons, he understood why. They'd given up hope, their eyes filled with despair.

Rye stopped the Black. "Who is in charge here?"

An older man stepped out. He looked like he hadn't eaten for days.

"Did you come to help us? Or are you just passing through like the others did?

"Others have been through here?"

"Last night, two men and a young woman came through. They took what they wanted and headed north."

"Duncan and Libbie." He didn't know who the third person would have been. "Where are you heading?"

"Leaving Montana and heading to Fort Laramie. We wound up in this canyon and have not been able to find a way out. Our guide took off with our money and other stuff as soon as we got here. We haven't eaten in a day or two."

Rye sized up the situation. "Why did you head out in the middle of winter? Why didn't you wait until spring?"

"We needed to get out of there."

"How many people do you have here?"

"Around twenty are still alive. A few died from starvation, but the ground's too hard to bury them."

"We'll have to find a way to get you to safety. There's a cabin a couple of hours south with some food and shelter. We'll have to load you onto horses to cross over that mountain pass."

"Thank you for coming to save us," a young boy said to Rye.

Rye surveyed the group for the first time. They'd all come out to see who had come. Hopeless faces in a harsh climate. Rye climbed off his horse and helped them ready the horses.

It took an hour, but Rye, with the help of those who still had the strength, helped prepare everyone for the trek. There were not enough horses, so several would be walking, and it would be difficult climbing up the snowy mountainside. He helped the older ladies onto the horses. They finally moved out.

Rye led the way up the mountain pass. A slow go, especially for the older folks barely hanging onto their mounts. After an hour's struggle, the last man made it to the forest.

Rye glanced at Jeremiah. "Do you think you can find

your way back to the cabin?"

"Yes sir."

"Head back and prepare the ladies."

"Will do."

Rye gave them a breather for about ten minutes. During that time several crawled off their horses and stretched out. The old man hobbled up to him.

"Thank you for saving our lives. My name is Nathan Hatcher."

"I'm glad I arrived when I did. I don't know how much longer you guys would have been able to hang on. You look pretty beat up."

"Yes. We're tired and we're hungry."

"Another hour or so, we'll get you to some warmth and food."

"Again, thank you."

Rye asked them to crawl back onto their horses. They moved out through the forest. Since Rye had been through there once before, he knew the trail and moved through more quickly than before. As soon as they came out of the forest, the snow started coming down. He quickened the pace to outrun the blizzard.

***

Blanche gazed to the north. She had slipped into her blouse and skirt with the boots she enjoyed wearing after Rye had left. She knew he enjoyed them also. Why was she even thinking about him?

The snow started coming down heavier. She hurried back into the cabin, which smelled wonderful. Isabelle and she had cooked up a stew thinking that Rye would want something warm.

Isabelle stopped stirring the pot. "Did you see him?"

"No, but I'm sure he'll be here soon."

At that moment Jeremiah came galloping into the cabin area and jumped off his horse. "Rye is coming with people who need help."

Christina had run out when he rode in. Blanche turned to Isabelle and asked her to get the place ready for needy guests. "Jeremiah, would you and Isabelle cut up some strips of cloth for any wounded?"

"Yes, ma'am."

***

The group struggled through the blinding snow toward the cabin. The temperature had dropped quickly. This major storm would hit them and hit them hard. Rye hoped he could get these people to the cabin before any of them froze to death. They'd make room for all of them.

Rye stopped. The whiteout made it difficult seeing behind and in front of him. He rode back and had the group tie ropes to each other's saddle horns in order to stay on the path, then tied a rope of his own to the one behind him and continued trudging ahead.

***

Blanche stood on the porch and started to worry. She didn't understand why. Christina grabbed some logs and laid them out a few yards in front of the cabin. It took a few moments before Christina could get a fire going. Their hope was Rye would see the fire and guide him to the cabin.

In the distance Blanche noticed a bit of movement in the trees. "They're coming. Isabelle. Hurry and get some blankets. The people need help." A large group led by Rye lumbered to the cabin and stopped.

Isabelle, Christina, and Jeremiah ran out the front door and started helping Rye help the people off the horses, starting with the older ladies. The other men who still had some strength helped others down.

Rye carried one of the older women into the cabin. He set her on the couch and Isabelle helped wrap a blanket around her. Rye went back out just as one of the men carried in a little girl.

Isabelle led him into her bedroom. She opened the blankets, and he laid her in the bed. She quickly covered her up. It took an hour before the last person made it into the cabin.

"Are you okay, Rye?" Blanche asked.

"Yeah, I'm fine. These people need some food. I'll take care of the horses if you can get them something to eat."

"I have some stew cooking so I will start with that," Blanche said. "I'm glad you're safe."

She hurried into the house while Rye battled the snow to take care of the horses. With Christina's help, Blanche carried bowls of stew to those in the living room.

A couple of the younger women came up to her. "Can we help?"

"Yes, please if you feel up to it. Isabelle can show you where everything is to dish out some stew. I may have to make more."

Blanche gave the pot of stew to Isabelle and asked her to distribute it to those who needed it. She turned back to help the ladies find the supplies they needed to make more. At least there would be enough to feed them all.

Christina turned when the door opened with a gale of wind. She stared at Rye's ice-filled face. He nodded at her.

Rye, Blanche, Christina, Jeremiah, Isabelle, and two ladies from the group fed everyone and made them comfortable. Meanwhile the wind howled outside the cabin.

In an hour, most of the group had fallen fast asleep. Isabelle slept next to her sister. Rye picked her up and carried her into her room. He tucked her into bed in the only room not in use. He did the same for Christina who opened her eyes and snuggled into him.

Only Blanche, Rye, and the two women who had helped with the meal were still awake, though the two ladies looked drained.

"Follow me," Blanche said. She led them to their bedroom. "Climb in with Isabelle and Christina and get some sleep. You'll stay warm."

"What about you two?"

“Don’t worry about us. We’ll be okay.”

One of the women touched her hand. “Thank you for what you have done for us.”

“You’re welcome.”

Blanche walked out of the room over to Rye. “Guess we’ll have to find somewhere to sleep tonight.”

“The floor will be fine.”

Blanche went toward the couch but stopped. She went over toward Bryce and slid down the wall next to him. “I’m glad you made it back safely.”

He glanced at her but didn’t speak. He pulled her near him and held her. Blanche fell asleep. Rye sat up against the wall with a rifle pointed toward the front door. He fell asleep in a few moments.

Chapter 24

Late the next morning, Rye opened his eyes, looked over at Blanche, and wondered. There was no doubt Blanche had been detailed to kill him, but not before he did something. Something he didn't know yet. He would find out. Even though he felt that, he also felt both of them didn't feel the way they had before.

Blanche stirred. She finally opened her eyes, then smiled up at Rye. "How long have you been looking at me?"

"Not long enough," he said. "How are you feeling?"

"I slept well. How about you?"

"I'm doing okay.' He peered around the room. "I don't know what to do with these people here."

She looked around the room. "They're very fortunate that you found them. The way they look I don't know if they could have survived another day."

Rye looked at her a moment too long.

"What?" she asked.

"When are you going to tell me why you are here? Or what this is all about?"

"I have no idea what you are talking about. I'm here because we escaped from our families and others."

Rye pushed up off the floor and went in the bedroom to check on Isabelle. Christina sat on the floor next to her. There were tears in her eyes. "What's wrong, Christina?"

She glanced up at him. "I don't know, Rye. Something bad is going to happen. I don't trust Blanche. I trust Libbie."

"Libbie is not here, Christina. I don't know where she is. I don't even know if she's alive. She is not the same Libbie."

"You care about Blanche?"

Rye didn't respond.

Christina stared up at the tall man. "Promise me one thing?"

"Anything."

"Don't ever stop looking for her. No matter what you believe or what you think about yourself, she is your heart and soul. Libbie Davis is the love of your life. She loves you, Rye. That I know."

Rye looked at her.

"One other thing."

"Just one?"

She smiled at him. "Please don't ever let anything happen to Isabelle. Protect her with your life. Promise me?"

"That I can promise," Rye said smiling back at her.

"Thank you."

Rye took Christina's hand and pulled her up. She walked out the door. Rye stared after her. What did she know that he didn't? He would find Libbie, but after that he didn't know.

***

Blanche whipped up some biscuits and beef. The aroma brought a few of the stranded wagon train members to the kitchen.

"Do you have coffee?" Nathan Hatcher asked.

"Sure do. It is just finishing up." She poured him a cup of coffee.

"Where is your husband?"

"Rye is outside checking the horses."

"Thank you for the coffee. Thank you for helping us."

"I'm just glad that Rye found you when he did."

Hatcher peered out the window. "Yes, he is a brave man. I will never be able to thank him enough."

Blanche smiled. "Mr. Hatcher, for some reason, that is what Rye finds himself doing...saving someone's life more times than not."

"I can see you love him."

"He is my life. I would do anything I could to save his life."

"I believe he would do the same for you."

"He has more than once."

"Thanks for the coffee."

Both looked at each other. Both knew each other had just lied.

***

More of the wagon train people woke up. Hatcher walked outside to talk to Rye. The snow had stopped, and the wind calmed down; it was still freezing, but not as cold as yesterday.

Hatcher found Rye walking one of the horses out of the barn to the river for water.

"How are you doing this morning?" he asked Hatcher.

"I'm much better. Thank you."

Rye continued walking toward the river. Hatcher followed him down.

"I don't think we could have lasted another day if you hadn't shown up"

"I'm just glad I arrived when I did.'

"I guess you want to know what happened."

"I reckon you'd say something when you were ready."

The two stopped while Rye watered the horse.

"Like I said our destination is Fort Laramie. Our guide decided he had enough of us. He must have had something else on his mind or wanted out of the situation."

"What happened?"

"He led us into that canyon, and the next morning he disappeared. I'd say about a week ago."

"He just up and vanished?"

"That's it. Actually, the woman left first. The man quickly followed once he found out she had left. He did tell us he'd be back, but he never showed up."

Rye didn't say anything else. It wasn't the whole story. It would be best to get these people out of here. "Is Laramie still your destination? You said a couple of days' drive from here."

"Yes, that's right," he said quickly.

Rye sensed something wasn't right. He couldn't place it but would be on the alert. He started toward the barn to take the horse back. "Let's get some breakfast and figure out the best way to get you to Laramie."

The two entered the house. Everyone was up and about. Not one person had lost their lives from the blizzard. After breakfast the talk turned toward leaving for Fort Laramie. Hatcher and his two sons did most of the talking.

Rye's mind wandered. Then it made sense. *Nathan Harkness*. During the war Duncan used to dabble in stealing women and selling them. Harkness or something like that was his connection. This man's name was Hatcher. Rye spoke up, "I will take you to Laramie. We'll saddle up and get started as soon as you are ready."

"We hope you will help us because we're not sure how to get there."

Rye didn't say anything. He asked Jeremiah to come out to the barn. He walked back out to get his horse ready. "Look after the girls, Jeremiah. Don't take any chances. I'm counting on you."

"I won't let you down."

"I know you won't. One other thing. There will be Cheyenne Dog Soldiers around at times. Don't be afraid. They'll help you watch over the women."

Chapter 25

Rye led them down out of the mountain. It took them most of the day to reach the plains. Once there was a straight shot to Laramie, he'd send this group on their way. One thing he did know—he'd return to Blanche and the kids as soon as he could.

He also figured that they would run into Marcus Duncan somewhere along the route. Until he killed him, that man would not let him live his life. It had to end soon. There'd been many opportunities, but Rye had hesitated in killing the man. He couldn't figure out why, but what he'd said at the cabin was true.

The caravan headed south, keeping the mountain range on the west side of the group. Rye pulled into an area that would protect them from the wind and provide good cover from anything that might come their way.

The group started fires and settled in for the evening. Rye slept near the horses so he could keep an eye on everything. Tomorrow they would be closer to Laramie, so it figured that would be the time Duncan would show up. Rye also noticed that the two women who were scared bedded down close to him, but not too close to cause suspicion.

A noise woke him up. Rye scrambled up and headed toward the noise, which came from the brush. One of the young men had ripped the clothes off of one of the women. Rye crept toward him, grabbed him from behind, and snapped his neck, killing him instantly. Hatcher's son.

The woman stared at him with terrified eyes.

"Don't worry. We'll get you and your friend out of this tomorrow. Go back to your bed and try to get some sleep. Be ready tomorrow. We'll take you to Laramie. You can tell your story to the authorities there."

The woman touched him on the arm. "Thank you. I am Beth. I will remember you." She ran out of the brush with her arms covering her breasts and quickly climbed into her bedroll.

The next morning the riders headed south again. Either Hatcher didn't care about his son or figured he'd left.

"Heartless bastard," Rye said to himself.

They had ridden another six days before Rye halted the group for lunch. Fort Laramie loomed in the distance. Rye couldn't make sense of it all. The women still looked scared. It wasn't until a mile or so from the fort that the women smiled for the first time. They rode up to Rye and thanked him for bringing them to safety.

Hatcher remained impassive. The cavalry detachment rode up and stopped to talk to Rye.

"Welcome," one of the men said, "I am so glad that you were able to find them and bring them to safety. We sent scouts out looking for them."

"Who are they?" he asked the lieutenant.

"Who are they? The women are the daughters of the colonel at the post. He's been searching for them for several weeks after they'd made the trip from up north."

The escort brought them into the fort. Hatcher joined Rye. "Thank you for your help." He started to walk away, then turned. "It isn't finished yet. I know you killed my boy." With a smirk the man walked away.

Rye crawled off his horse. The fort had a lot of activities. A wagon train sat outside the fort. Rye had to turn twice when he saw a man and a woman who resembled Christina and Isabelle. *It couldn't be.* He had to know for sure. Rye found the wagon master and asked their names.

"They came with us from Abercrombie," he said. "They lost all three of their children—two girls and a boy—to the damn Sioux."

Christina's parents. He had to tell her mother and father they were in the mountains. It would be difficult because he loved the trio—the family he had never had. But he needed to do the right thing. And Rye did the right thing. He ambled up to them. "Sir, ma'am, I know this is going to be a shock, but your children are still alive in the mountains."

They both broke into tears, and the woman clung to him. "Are you sure?"

"Yes, the little girl is a brave trooper. She has saved many people."

"And the other two?"

"They are there also."

Both were in tears. "Could you take us to them?"

"That I can do. Are you part of the train?"

"Yes. It can't leave until spring."

"That's still several months away. Let's go see the colonel and see if he could spare an escort to take you up there and bring you back."

The woman grabbed his arm. "Thank you so much."

"I'm just glad the children's parents are still alive."

After a few moments of conversation with the colonel, he called in a captain. "Ben, please saddle up your men and follow Mr. Tyler up into the mountains to get this couple's children."

"Yes sir," he said and saluted the colonel. He stopped and looked at Rye for a moment before leaving. Rye did a double take. The man in the photo of his family he'd never seen before. Strange because he thought he knew his family. Then he remembered hearing about two men he had never seen.

Rye had one last thing to do before they headed out in the morning. He went into the post store, purchased an item, and had them wrap it, then he placed it into his saddlebag.

The next morning, they hit the trail early. The temperature had fallen during the night. Rye had been used to the snow and had an inkling it would snow again before they started their trek up the mountain.

After a week of traveling, the group reached the mountains. Rye stared in awesome wonder at the beauty.

The captain broke the silence. "Where do we go from here?"

Rye didn't answer right away. He pointed up the mountain. "We should be there by the end of the day."

"Then let's move out," the captain stated. The group slowly went up the mountain with Rye leading the way, one of the easier climbs Rye had been associated with in his short time in the mountains.

Close to nightfall the group finally reached the mountain cabin.

***

Isabelle heard the horses. "He's back," she said running out of the cabin.

Blanche put down her towel and ran out after her. She smiled at Rye as he came up the draw, but it quickly turned to fear when she saw the man riding beside him. "Oh my God," she said to herself. "It can't be."

Isabelle came over to Rye's horse and he pulled her up. "Got a surprise for you, little one."

"I like surprises."

"You will love this one."

"What is it?"

She turned at a scream and saw a woman running toward her. "Mom, is that you?" Isabelle stayed on Rye's horse. She looked at her father. Christina and Jeremiah ran out the door when they heard the screaming. Rye stared at Isabelle. Why didn't she get off the horse?

Blanche came up and stood beside Rye. "I'm glad you made it back safely," she said. Then she looked at the captain. He smiled at her.

176

"Blanche, is it?"

"Yes."

Rye looked at the two of them. They knew each other. He heard her welcome all of them into the cabin. She brushed past Rye with the two kids and their parents.

The captain dismissed the troops. Before Blanche stepped into the house, she asked the captain to join them for supper.

"I would be glad to," he said smiling once more.

Rye turned to take care of his horse. Isabelle stayed near him. "What is it, Isabelle?"

"I don't want to leave with them. I want to stay with you."

"Those are your parents."

"No, they left me. They abandoned us. You stayed with us."

Blanche had told him not to be too long for supper. He convinced Isabelle to at least come in for the meal.

Something didn't seem right. Or maybe the long trek tired him out. He chalked it up to the second thought. He heard all the laughing inside the cabin with the kids and their family. The captain and Blanche seemed to be having a good time also. Rye stepped outside the cabin and sat on the porch. Isabelle stayed near him.

The captain and Blanche stepped outside together. It could just be Blanche being Blanche, but again something didn't click with Rye in this situation.

After the captain said goodbye to her and Rye, he joined his men. Blanche walked back inside, and Rye followed. Why had she stopped to glance back at the captain? Rye smoothed Isabelle's hair as she snuggled next to him and fell asleep.

Christina came out and sat on Rye's other side. She took his hand. "Rye, although they are our parents, please don't let them take Isabelle with them."

"What are you talking about?"

"They didn't want her."

Rye stared at her. "Are you kidding?"

"I'm not. She loves you. You promised me that you would take care of her."

"Yes, I did, but we're talking about your parents."

Tears rolled down Christina's eyes. "Please, don't let them take her."

The next morning, everyone woke up early, ready to go back down the mountain. Tears flowed. Isabelle would not let go of Rye.

"Isabelle, let's go." her father said.

Isabelle peered up at Rye. Rye took a big breath and turned back to their ma and pa. "Ma'am, if Isabelle leaves, you will never make it out of this mountain."

"What are you talking about?" Blanche asked.

Rye explained about the edict from the Cheyenne Dog Soldiers. Isabelle's parents stared at each other for a moment. "If that's the case, we should leave her here," the mother said.

Christina came over to her sister. "Isabelle, please look after Rye. He will need it."

"I promise, big sister. I'll miss you."

"You're safe now, sweetheart." The two hugged. Christina turned to Rye and kissed him on the cheek. "Thank you. Take care of her."

Christina climbed on a horse and rode near Rye once more. "Remember what I said? Things aren't always as they seem."

"You don't have to worry about me, young lady. You are with family now."

Christina turned to her mother and father. "Not really, but at least Isabelle is safe." She rode away. Rye didn't know what to think.

The captain rode up to Blanche. "Ma'am, if you are willing, you could come to Fort Laramie with us. It would be much safer than up here."

Blanche glanced at Rye and without hesitation said, "I feel safe here."

A vein appeared in the captain's neck and he stared at her for a moment too long, then he smiled, turned, and led the men down the mountain. Blanche's lip quivered as she stared after him.

"Are you okay?" Rye asked her.

"Yes." She turned and walked into the cabin.

Isabelle tugged on Rye's hand, and he bent down to her. She whispered in his ear, "she's a big liar. She wants that captain."

"I don't think so, little one." They went in a few moments later. "Are you sure you're okay?" Rye peered at Blanche.

She turned to him, tears in her eyes. "I would rather be alone right now."

Rye nodded and headed out to the porch. Lowering himself onto the step, he started processing all that had happened over the last few days. Christina was right about appearances. The captain had spooked Blanche.

Blanche stepped out the door. "Walk with me, Rye?" she asked, taking his hand. He pulled himself up and strolled with her down to the river. They ambled along the bank before anyone spoke.

"This is so peaceful," Rye said. "I want it to remain like this, but I don't know if that can happen."

"What do you mean?"

"They will be coming for me. You should have gone with the captain."

"Don't think like that. I've told you before you are the strongest person I've ever known."

"Thank you for saying that. I'm being realistic. The Sioux are out there, and once they find us, they'll be coming after us in swarms. Then there is Duncan. You really don't know how ruthless he is. And don't forget Hatcher. The Blackfeet have talked about Confederates in these mountains. They will know who I am. Finally, there is the sergeant and his group. They didn't disappear. They're out there somewhere."

She linked her arm in his. "You are to blame for that."

"What do you mean?"

Blanche smiled at him. "You had to be some kind of hero and find me in that slough. That started everything."

The two turned to look at the sun setting in the west. Blanche lifted Rye's arm and pulled it over her shoulder. "That sunset is so beautiful. It makes everything worth it."

***

She dreamed about a man in a cavalry uniform and the end coming closer to the man standing next to her.

Rye looked at her. "Blanche, why do you continue to play this game?"

Before she could answer, a noise came from the river. Rye ran toward the river bank with Blanche on his heels. He looked down and saw the face of a young girl who had apparently fallen off her horse into the river.

Rye bent over and scooped her up while Blanche grabbed the horse. She was several inches shorter than Blanche, had dark hair, and dressed in what looked like a Blackfoot dress.

Blanche put the horse in the corral while Rye carried the young girl into the house. Blanche hurried in after him.

Isabelle came out of her room. "What happened? I heard a scream. She can go into my bedroom."

Rye laid her on the bed and started checking to see what had happened. He found a bullet hole on the left side of her chest.

"Quick, get some water heated up. We have to get that bullet out or she'll not survive."

Blanche did as asked. In a few moments, Rye took a sterilized knife and dug into the bullet hole. The girl didn't stir. It took him a few moments, but Rye found the bullet and dug it out. Isabelle stood beside Rye, wiping off the girl's face with a warm rag.

After he took the bullet out, Blanche treated the wound and wrapped it up. She stayed with the girl until her breathing had steadied. Before Blanche left the bedroom, she peered at Isabelle. "Can you stay with her?"

"I'll stay near her in case she wakes up, and I'll come and get you if she needs you."

Rye stood outside the cabin behind a pillar staring off into the dark.

Blanche joined him. "What do you think happened?"

"I'm not sure. She has a Blackfoot dress, but she's a white girl. And I'm also not sure about the bullet I pulled out of her."

"What do you mean?"

"It's safe to say a white man tried to kill her, but Hatcher and Duncan have run with the Blackfeet, so it may be a Blackfoot also. It's hard to tell."

"What are you going to do?"

"I'm going to stay up for a while just to make sure she's okay. You look tired. Maybe you should get some sleep."

"I am tired. It's been a long few days."

"Good night."

"Good night." She smiled and walked back into the cabin.

Chapter 26

Rye walked into the bedroom where the young woman slept. Isabelle had fallen asleep in a chair next to her. He sat on the bed beside the young woman. "Who are you? What happened to you?" He felt her forehead. Her fever had gone down. He covered her up, closed the door, and sat on the couch. Thinking about the situation, he fell asleep.

It felt like he had just fallen asleep when Blanche shook him. "Did you sleep out here all night?"

"I checked on the girl, then must have fallen asleep. Where else would I sleep?"

"That's true. Hopefully someday that will change."

They both jumped at the scream.

Rye raced into the bedroom. The young girl sat up. Her terrified eyes darted around the room. Rye sat on the side of the bed, trying to calm her down. He talked to her in a soft voice, hoping that would help her. Isabelle stood behind him, peeking around his shoulder.

The young woman said something to him in the Blackfoot tongue. Blanche glanced at Rye not knowing what she said. She said it again. Finally, Rye spoke to her, trying to help her understand that he did not know her language.

The girl frowned at him. In English, she said, "I have seen you in my dreams."

Rye and Blanche looked at each other, wide-eyed.

"What do you mean?" Blanche asked.

"I am Black Elk's daughter. You spared no one." She

rolled over and fell back to sleep. Rye checked her forehead. Her temperature had increased.

"We had better cool her down." Blanche quickly walked out to the kitchen, grabbed a cool, wet cloth, and sat on her bed to try to break the fever. Rye left the room and sat on the porch bench.

***

When Blanche came out, Rye was staring toward the mountains. She sat down next to him. "Her fever has broken."

Rye didn't say anything.

"Do you know what is happening?"

"I have no clue," Rye responded. He turned to her. "You knew the captain."

"I don't know what you're talking about."

"You know exactly what I'm talking about. I have a feeling he is one of my long-lost brothers."

Blanche didn't respond.

The girl continued sleeping throughout the morning. Isabelle stayed near her. Blanche made it a point to wake her up. She struggled, but the young girl finally sat up in bed. At first the girl refused the soup, but Blanche calmly told her that she needed to eat to build her strength. Blanche fed her a couple of spoonfuls of soup. After the third one, the girl eyed the room.

"Where is he?"

"Do you mean Rye?"

She looked at Blanche with a frown.

"Rye is the man who rescued you earlier."

She nodded.

"He is around."

"Please do not let him leave me."

Blanche continued to feed her the soup. She would talk to her more as soon as she had regained her strength. After finishing the soup, Blanche helped her back down and covered her up. "You need to get more rest."

"My name is Little Deer. Thank you." She fell back to sleep.

Blanche stared at her for a few moments and then went in search of Rye. He wasn't anywhere in sight. Blanche sighed and headed to the kitchen to make some lunch for the three of them. She thought about what had just happened. Blanche had no idea what to think about this young woman or how she fit into the complicated scenario. Of course, it may not be anything. But she had a feeling this girl would cause problems for Rye. That might be a good thing.

A few moments later, Rye came into the cabin. Blanche spun around when the door opened.

"Everything okay?" she asked.

"Yes, I fed the horses and doubled back to check the signs of where the woman had come from."

"Anything?"

"Just her horse trail for at least a mile back. I don't know how she got separated from her tribe or how she ended up in this area."

"What do you think?" Blanche asked.

"I don't know what to think. My suspicions are she's part of your so-called plan that you may not even know about."

Blanche flinched. "Well why don't you turn that mind off and have some lunch."

They sat down and ate sandwiches and coffee. Isabelle joined them a few moments later.

"She seems to be feeling better."

"I think she'll be okay," Blanche said.

Rye glanced up. "Where do you think she came from?"

"I don't know. But more importantly, who shot her?"

"That's a question I hope she can answer. But why didn't they follow her?"

"What do you think she meant when she said you spared none of them?"

Rye frowned. "I have no idea. This is all just plain

strange. A girl is shot. She ends up at this cabin. No one follows her. It doesn't add up."

"We'll figure it out, Rye."

"When will it end?"

Blanche chuckled.

"What?" he asked.

"Maybe it's just your charm."

He rolled his eyes, Rye took the plates to the kitchen, and placed them in the sink. He started to put water in to wash the dishes.

Blanche touched his arm. "I can do that. Why don't you go out and see if you can find something else to make sense of what is happening here?"

"I guess I can do that." He turned to Isabelle. "Stay with the young girl. I'm counting on you to take care of her."

She smiled. "My pleasure."

He started to turn away. Blanche stopped him. "Be careful," she said softly.

"I hope you mean that." The hard lines framing his mouth stunned her.

***

Rye made it to the mile-marker like before. He stopped and studied the area, sensing the eyes on him. Rye would be ready.

Something in the trees drew him toward them. As he reached the edge, he stopped. Tracks led in, but they didn't follow the young girl. This was the way that she had come. He walked into the trees. The snow became deeper the higher he climbed. Another twenty minutes and he came to a beautiful lake. Rye stopped, his mouth agape. Right here in his backyard, all this beauty. And in all this beauty, death.

"I thought all Indians moved quietly," Rye said as he swung around with his gun pointed at the Blackfoot.

"That is a lake where all of our maidens go swimming and refresh themselves," Black Elk said.

Rye put his pistol back in his holster. He waited for him

to continue speaking.

"Here they came and took everyone, but Little Deer. She got away, but not until they shot her."

"Why have you not come for her?" Rye asked.

"She is safer with you."

"You are wrong there. I have the Confederates, Union, Blackfeet, and Sioux all wanting my scalp. How would she be safe with me?"

"You are a killer; there is no doubt about that. But more importantly, your heart is pure, the heart of the woman you love even more so. That is why Little Deer is in the best place possible. You three will be connected for the remainder of each other's lives."

"She belongs with her family, the Blackfeet."

Black Elk looked around the lake. "There is beauty out there, but that is ending. In part because of the white soldiers but also because of the friction amongst our tribes. I will not live much longer. I will be killed. But I will die knowing that my only daughter will be protected."

"And why would I do that? I just want to live in peace. I'm tired of fighting."

"I know, Rye Tyler. Here is something you don't know. That girl is special. But, I think you know that. There are people who will go to any length to do away with her or marry her because of who she really is."

Rye looked at him with narrowed eyes.

"I can tell you are confused. You have figured out she is not Blackfoot. But when you find out who her father is, you will know how important she is."

"I know she is an important woman, but I'm not sure who her father is. I'm assuming you are not going to tell me who she is."

"It is not my place. You will find out soon enough." Black Elk turned to ride away.

"One question for you."

Black Elk stopped.

"What did she mean when she said that I would spare no one?"

"That I cannot say. You will know soon enough. The one thing I will say is keep her close. She needs you to survive. She will also protect you and anyone who cares for you."

"I will protect her."

Black Elk stared at him. "There was no doubt you would. That is who you are." He disappeared into the trees.

Chapter 27

After Blanche finished doing the dishes, she checked in on Little Deer. Still sleeping, but much more peaceful than before. Isabelle sat next to her.

"Why are you really here at this place?" Blanche asked.

"I feel safe with Rye. I don't feel safe with my mother and father. They don't want me. You don't want me either."

Blanche didn't respond. She could relate to how Isabelle felt about being safe. She sat there for a few moments with Little Deer. After that she walked out onto the porch looking toward the north. Hopefully, Rye had discovered some answers.

Someone or something was hidden in the trees. She returned inside the house and grabbed the rifle that Rye had set by the door. When she came back out, she pointed the rifle toward Marcus Duncan and Libbie.

"Rye has rubbed off on you, Blanche."

"What do you want?"

"We came for the Indian girl."

"Don't think so. She can't be moved."

"Let me be the judge of that."

Marcus started to climb off the horse but stopped when Blanche fired a shot near him.

***

Rye stopped and glanced back toward the cabin. He took off running fast and hard. He wasn't too far away, but a bullet didn't take that long.

***

Blanche kept the rifle trained on them." Marcus, you and Libbie need to turn around and head back where you come from. In fact, never set foot near this cabin ever again."

"Do you really believe that you and Rye are going to live here in peace? Rye will figure it out sooner or later," Libbie said.

"Only if you tell him. It's none of your business. Now, please leave and never come back. I don't want to kill my sister. I would rather someone else do it. But if I have to I will."

Libbie glared at her. "Why don't you let him go?"

"Maybe you don't know the significance of what's going on here, sister."

"You may convince him to marry you, but he'll never love you. His heart will always belong to me. I also know that the girl in the cabin will turn against Rye sooner or later."

"Maybe my feelings have changed."

Libbie's eyes widened.

***

Rye had made it back. He went into the other room to check on the Indian girl. She had not moved. Rye returned and sat down next to Blanche.

She looked up at him.

"They came for Little Deer."

"I know. I ran into her father, Black Elk, out on the trail. He asked me to protect her."

Blanche shifted to face him. "We have to protect her. She doesn't deserve any of this. She is just a fifteen-year-old girl."

Rye's brow furrowed. "How do you know her age?"

"I'm just guessing, but she doesn't look much younger than Christina."

"We need to get her well, and while that is happening,

prepare the cabin for an onslaught of people coming after her. From what her father says, she is pretty special."

"Her father?"

"Yes, Black Elk. The chief is her father. This is his only daughter. And there are others who want to see her dead."

"We'll do what we can to protect her by any means." Blanche peered up at him. "Why did you lie about Isabelle to her parents?"

"I did not lie."

Both turned at the sound of a Cheyenne Dog Soldier. Around him were other Dog Soldiers. "She is sacred to Rye Tyler. Just as Little Deer is."

"Why would a Dog Soldier want anything to do with Blackfeet?"

The Dog Soldier didn't say anything for a moment. "You do not know what is about to happen, White Man. This country is about to be covered with blood. The Blackfeet are our hated enemy, but we will fight with them. Or it will be the end of our nation. You and that girl in there will play a part in it all."

They turned and rode into the woods. Rye and Blanche peered at each other, not sure what to say.

***

Little Deer slept throughout the day and evening and woke up early the next morning. Rye had been sleeping on the couch when she walked into the room. She peered down at him and smiled. He looked so full of peace, something she wished that she had.

Rye looked up at her. "I see you are doing better."

"I feel much better. Thank you for helping me."

Rye stretched and stood. "I'm going to check your forehead to see if your fever has gone down."

She didn't move. "I trust you. I feel safe around you."

Rye put his hand on her forehead. "The fever has broken, and you are looking much better."

Little Deer looked over at Blanche, who was asleep at

190

the kitchen table. "Your woman?"

"No. Her heart is for someone else."

"I don't believe that is true."

"Are you hungry?"

"Yes, I am."

"Why don't you sit at the table and I will make you some eggs?"

"You can cook?'

"Yes. I have been alone most of my life."

"In my world, a man would never do such a thing. All they do is kill men and beat women."

"I'm sorry to hear that." Rye scrambled up some eggs.

Blanche had awakened at the smell of bacon. "Good morning."

"Good morning," he replied.

Isabelle came out a few moments later. Blanche smiled at her and said good morning. She smiled back. A few moments later the four sat at the table eating breakfast.

Little Deer slowly ate her breakfast. "It is good to eat. Your man cooks well."

Blanche smiled at her. "Rye is pretty handy to have around."

Little Deer smiled back at her.

"After breakfast I'll need to check your wound," Rye said.

After they completed the meal, Rye came over to her. "I'm going to have to pull your blouse down a bit to look at the wound."

She didn't flinch when he touched her shoulder. Rye probed around the area with his fingers. "It looks like it is going to heal properly. You are a lucky young lady."

Little Deer pulled her shirt up.

Rye sat back down at the table next to her. "Can you tell us what happened?"

She hesitated.

Rye put his hand on her shoulder. "It's okay. You can

talk to us."

She nodded. "All fifteen of us were swimming in the frozen lake, having fun, and then all of a sudden they came swarming out of the trees shooting and hollering."

"Do you know who?" Rye asked.

"White men like you. They had a different color of suit. A gray suit."

Blanche and Rye stared at each other. Little Deer noticed. "You know them?"

"We know of them," Blanche said.

Little Deer went on with the story. "I did not know what to do. I remembered my father telling me if anything ever happened to come to this cabin. A man here would save me. I climbed onto a horse and headed up the mountain through the trees. They shot at me and one hit me. Then a man protected me. He grabbed my horse and led me to a lake. He laid me on the bank and washed my wound. He told me to find you and come here. The men in gray rode up, and the man ran away. I passed out and don't know what happened until I opened my eyes and saw your face," she said looking at Rye. "I know I am safe because I have seen your face many times in my dreams. You have always protected me."

Blanche patted her hand. "You are safe here. You can stay in the bedroom that you were sleeping in until you are ready to go home."

She stood up. "I will never go home. My dreams told me that my father would die as soon as I left, and I would have no home. Rye and I will be connected until one of us dies."

Blanche smiled. "You have a home here. He will protect you like he has protected Isabelle and me."

Little Deer stared at the man who was heading out the door. "I know, but it will not be easy."

Blanche nodded. "It has never been easy."

Chapter 28

Rye sat on the porch looking to the north. He enjoyed the peace and solitude, even when everything seemed in disarray. Watching Isabelle was no problem, but with the white girl in the cabin he had no idea what would come next. He knew it wouldn't be good. What he had to do was go on the offense. First thing would be to get the lay of the land. He had been at least an hour or so east and south but not north or west. Tomorrow he would head north toward Blackfeet country.

The young girl looked better. She and Isabelle would be a help to Blanche. Rye had to find out if the Blackfeet chief had met his death like he predicted. If Black Elk did, Little Deer would not be safe either.

Once his mind was made up, he walked out to the barn area and started getting things ready. He would talk to Blanche later in the cabin.

When he walked in, Blanche was chatting with the white girl and Isabelle as they prepared supper. Blanche turned and smiled at him, but it quickly went away. "You are going after them?"

Rye looked at her. "Something has to be done. This can't go on forever."

"But why you, Rye? Why do you have to risk your life?"

"Who else is it going to be?" Blanche turned away and continued cooking supper.

***

The young girl looked at both of them. She didn't understand the feelings the two had for each other. She went over to help Blanche. Little Deer saw the tears streaming down the woman's face. She took her hand. Blanche turned to her. "Rye is right. He is the only one who can stop it."

"I have seen him many times in my dreams. Each time he is there to protect me."

***

Blanche stared at her, and then turned when Rye walked back in. No one spoke much during supper. Little Deer and Isabelle went to bed early after supper. A couple of hours later Rye and Blanche followed.

Blanche rose early the next morning, putting together a couple of days' meals for Rye. Little Deer had risen early to help. After breakfast, Rye held Isabelle tightly.

"I will return, Isabelle. I promise."

The young girl hugged him tight. "Please be careful and come back."

"I will, little one," he said, rubbing her hair. "You watch after Little Deer."

Isabelle smiled and nodded.

Rye started to walk out the door. He turned and looked at Blanche. Tears streamed down her eyes.

"Please come back?"

***

Rye turned and walked toward his horse. He climbed on it, looked one last time at Blanche. "Are you sure you want me to come back? I believe your heart is with that captain." He tipped his hat at her and headed toward the north.

Blanche watched him riding off, stunned at what he had just said. Had he figured it out? How could he? He didn't realize she didn't feel the same as before.

Little Deer came out and took Blanche's hand. "He will return."

Blanche glanced at her. "I hope so."

The two stood on the porch until Rye disappeared over

the mountain. Isabelle stood off to the side.

***

They weren't the only three that watched Rye leave. Hatcher and his sons witnessed the whole thing. He had wanted the tall, young woman since he saw her. She would bring good money. And the younger woman would be an added bonus. They would bide their time and see what Tyler did.

***

Blanche turned to walk back into the house. Little Deer stood out for a few moments with Isabelle. Something wasn't right. She would not say anything to Blanche at this moment, but she would keep an eye out for her. Little Deer would protect Blanche until Rye returned. She turned to Isabelle. "Why do you care about Rye?"

"Like you, he saved my life. I feel safe around him."

Little Deer did not say anything.

***

This time when Rye reached the site of the massacre, he quickly rode past it. He had no idea what he would see over the next mountain, Rye slowly made the climb over the next mountain and the next. He went over at least three mountain passes before the plains sat in front of him along with an encampment of men. There must be at least fifty of them camped in military fashion—Rebel and Union soldiers, alike.

Rye climbed off the Black and surveyed the encampment. To the right was a stockade with Indian women and children packed into it. What was going on? The men were holding slaves here.

Rye led his horse around the peaks to keep from being seen. As he got closer to the plains, fortress sentries spread out around for at least a mile in each direction, but none on this side of the encampment. It dawned on him that they felt that no one in their right mind would come over the mountain after them. Many had said Rye fit that description.

Rye took a seat and continued to scout the area. This many men could do a ton of damage in this neck of the woods, but Rye had no idea what this all meant. Blanche probably knew about this setup and what plan had been devised. He needed to discover what that plan consisted of.

He had heard Marcus Duncan talking about needing him to make the plan work. Rye's hunch was it had to do with the gold bullion and fighting in the West. Sooner or later the Confederacy would fall. Just too many men and arms in the North.

He continued watching throughout the day. At one point, soldiers marched a group of Indians out of the crudely made stockade, lined them up, and shot them. Rye looked on in horror. He also noticed something or someone to the left outside of the fortress. When it grew dark, he would go down and take a closer look.

***

Blanche and Isabelle sat out on the porch and looked to the north. With the sun going down, the chill in the air made them shiver. The wind and dropping temperatures made it chilly. Little Deer came out the door with a blanket and sat down by the three. They cuddled into the blanket.

Little Deer broke the silence. "What do you think of when you sit out here?"

"Oh, lots of things," Blanche said.

"Do you think about your husband all the time?"

"He is not my husband. But no, I don't think about him all the time. I think about what to do with this place."

"What do you mean?"

"I mean I want to make some kind of business out of it."

"What is business?"

"It is something that a person does to make money. Something that I had been good at before I came here."

"Then why did you stop doing that?"

"I fell in love with a man several years ago. He left and then came back, and I fell in love once more."

"Is it Rye?"

Blanche shook her head.

"Then why are you with Rye?"

"It is complicated. I do know my feelings have changed toward him."

***

Isabelle looked at the women. She didn't say anything, but even as a ten-year-old, she knew Blanche was waiting for an opportunity to dispose of Rye. Isabelle would do what she could to help him.

Little Deer spoke up again. "He does not want you to start a business?"

"I'm sure he'll be supportive of whatever I do."

"Then why don't you do it? Start a business."

"Partly because I don't know what to do."

"You are a good cook. And you have space in your cabin. Maybe it could be a hunting lodge or something like that."

"That is an idea, but I'm not sure many people come up this way."

"Oh yes. They come through in the spring and all during the summer. Winter time not so much."

"That's something to think about."

Neither said anything for a few moments. Blanche finally said, "Little Deer, do you truly believe that your father will not survive?"

"Yes, I believe he is dead or will be dead."

"Why do you believe that?"

"It is in my dreams. Dreams are powerful among our people."

"I hope you are wrong."

"Why?"

"Because I would like to meet him. He must be a good man because you are a strong woman...much like Rye."

"And much like you, Blanche," she said.

Blanche smiled at her. "I don't want to scare you, Little

Deer, but I believe we are being watched."

Little Deer was quiet and stared ahead, then said, "I know we are being watched, but I made it my mission to protect you. You saved my life."

Blanche put her arms around the two girls. "We will protect each other."

***

After the darkness fell, Rye slowly worked his way down the mountain toward where a man hanged on a pole. It took him around fifteen minutes to reach the spot. He stopped in shock. Hanging on the makeshift cross was Black Elk. Still alive.

Rye quickly moved toward him, cutting him down from the wooden stakes. He flung the chief's unconscious body over his shoulders and raced back up the mountain. Rye struggled, but he finally made it to his horse as the sun started to rise. It would only be a few moments before they would notice Black Elk gone.

Rye tied Black Elk onto his horse still unconscious, barely alive. He would do everything he could to save this man for Little Deer's sake. A clamor came from down below. The Blackfeets' chants grew louder and louder. They knew their leader had died or would die.

Rye pulled out his gun and shot into the sky, scattering horses into the valley and allowing the Blackfeet captives to scatter into the mountains. The white men chased after their spooked horses.

Rye rode in the direction of the cabin. The Indians would be combing the area trying to find their leader. Rye led the horse up over the mountain, hoping that he would have enough lead on them to reach the cabin. He didn't know if he could make a stand. Right now he had to get the Blackfeet chief to a safer spot.

With Black Elk, Rye made slow progress over the mountain passes. It took him an hour to complete the first pass. He stopped long enough to let the horse rest but kept an eye on his backtrail. They had not found it, but it would only be a matter of time and they'd be coming. Rye also knew it would be unpredictable odds. On top of that, the snow started to fall. It would hide the tracks, but it also would slow Rye down. At this point he could make it back by nightfall if lucky.

***

Blanche had been feeding the horses when she heard the first sound. "My, my. I hoped that I would run into you once more."

She turned around and calmly said, "Mr. Hatcher. What a pleasant surprise. What brings you back up to this area of the country?"

"Well, we just happen to be heading back to Montana and thought maybe we could get something to eat. I remembered your cooking was pretty good."

"If you give me a moment to finish feeding the horses, I'll round you something up."

Hatcher grabbed her arm and twisted her back toward him. "There is no need to do that. I want a little more than just food from you."

Blanche pulled away from him. "I wouldn't do that if I were you."

"And why not?"

"Rye will be back soon, and you had better be gone before he's back."

"I plan on being gone, but I also plan on taking you with me. As pretty as you are, you'll bring plenty of money for me and the boys." He stopped for a moment. "It's kind of interesting though that you are out here in the wilderness with a killer, while back at the fort, a man claims to be married to you and loves you."

"I don't know what you are talking about." Her response threw him off guard. Blanche didn't hesitate. She kneed Hatcher in the groin and ran toward the door. The other two tried to grab at her, but she was too quick for them and slid past. She ran toward the house.

"Get her, damn it," Hatcher said. "I want her. Rip her clothes off. I'm going to bed her until she screams for mercy. Then you two can do the same."

Blanche ran as fast as her long legs would take her. She made it to the door. Little Deer opened it for her and she scrambled through it. Little Deer slammed it shut and bolted it.

"You run pretty fast."

Blanche didn't say anything. She scrambled around the house to make sure everything had been locked up including windows and the back doors. Isabelle brought some rifles out for them. Blanche knew the rifles were loaded. It would not be easy for them to get to either of the women. The hope was they could hold off until Rye returned. The problem was she didn't know when that would happen.

***

Rye continued struggling through the snow. The Blackfoot chief still hadn't awakened. Darkness had fallen, and they still had a ways to go.

He stopped to take a break. As he did a scout came at him with a knife. Rye turned just in time. Rye jumped to the side and grabbed him from behind. He quickly killed him. When Rye saw his face, he gasped. It wasn't a Confederate soldier but a Sioux warrior dressed in a Confederate uniform. Sioux fighting with Confederates? Worse than he thought. Rye quickly gathered the horse's reins and headed south once more.

***

Blanche had fallen asleep and awakened when one of the men plowed through the window. Blanche aimed the rifle and pulled the trigger. She missed. The man grabbed her and pulled her down onto the floor. Little Deer jumped on him and stabbed him with a knife. He screeched and rolled over.

Blanche stood up and shot him through the head, killing him instantly. The other two tried to break through the front door. Flames licked under the door, and the room filled with smoke. Blanche grabbed Little Deer's hand and ran toward the back room. She found Isabelle huddled in a corner. The room would be difficult to break into. The only way they could get in would be by burning them out. They didn't want that to happen because Hatcher wanted her.

Blanche looked at Isabelle. "Good girl."

***

Hatcher burst through the front door after the fire had cooled down. He looked down at his dead boy and let out a scream that scared even his son.

"Find them. I want that woman alive."

They searched through the house and finally were outside the room where the women huddled in the corner. Blanche trained the rifle at the door. She would shoot until her last breath. The two men tried to break through the door.

"Go out and get the axe I saw in the barn."

***

Minutes later, the son came out of the barn with the axe and stopped.

"I told you that you wouldn't live if you tried to hurt Blanche or Isabelle."

The man squealed. "My father. He wants the older woman."

The last words he said. Rye slit his throat. He quickly headed into the cabin. Hatcher continued to beat down the door. He stopped when he felt eyes upon him. Rye motioned him away with his pistol. The man slowly backed away.

He looked scared. "You don't know who that woman is in there. I know I'm going to die, but she will be your destruction." Rye fired all six shots into the man's brain killing him instantly with the first shot. He made sure with the other five. Rye kicked in the door, and Blanche fired shot after shot. Rye had to duck out of the way to keep from getting hit. "Okay, Blanche. Don't kill me."

Blanche jumped up and ran out the door. Rye sat there

on the floor. "Did I hit you?"

He smiled at her. "I am going to have to teach you to be a better shot."

She didn't say anything more. Blanche started kissing him all over.

"Hey, stop and let me up."

She stopped. "What happened to Hatcher? Is he dead?"

Rye pointed at the floor. "He won't be hurting any woman again. We have to get outside and quickly." He looked for Isabelle. The young girl stood to the side out of the way. He held out his hand. She took it. "I'm glad you're safe, little one."

She smiled and hugged him.

Rye went outside. He picked up Black Elk, swung him over his shoulder, and brought him into the house. He took him into the back bedroom and laid him on the bed. "He is still alive, but I don't know how and for how long."

Little Deer came out and saw her father. Tears streamed down her eyes. "Is he dead?"

"No, Little Deer. He is still alive. I don't know how long he will survive. They worked him over fairly well."

Blanche sprang into action returning with a cool cloth to wipe him down. She gave them to Little Deer who started that job. Blanche scurried back to the kitchen to cook something.

Rye came over and touched her shoulder. She turned to him. "They will be coming."

"Who?"

"Confederates and Sioux."

"Oh, my. How long?

"Maybe a few days. There will be too many to hold off."

"What do we do?"

"Try to get Black Elk as healthy as we can and then lead them on a wild goose chase into the mountains. I'll fight them on their terms."

"What about us?"

"I will take you to a safe place and will start picking them off one by one."

Blanche touched his arm. "Do it."

"Let's get him ready to move. If we don't get him out of here by the end of the day, we won't survive."

Blanche brought some soup to Black Elk. Little Deer fed him. While she did, Blanche whispered to her, "We have to get him up and out of here as soon as we can. They will be coming for us."

"What will we do?"

"Rye will take care of us."

"What does that mean?"

"Rye is adept at this type of warfare. He is going to fight them Sioux-style, something the Confederates won't suspect. But he needs to take us somewhere safe."

"I will do my part."

"I know you will. We all will."

Rye came in and asked about Black Elk.

"Still no sign of waking up."

"I don't think we can wait much longer. You need to take off."

"What are you talking about, Rye?"

"Fort Laramie. Go there and bring back the soldiers. Take Black Elk with you."

"You are insane."

Rye smiled. "You've said that several times in the short time I've known you. Take Little Deer, Isabelle, and get going. You can make it in a week or so." He tied Black Elk onto one of the horses securely. She climbed on her horse. "And Blanche...you, Isabelle, and Little Deer, stay at Fort Laramie."

Blanche looked at him.

Rye repeated. "Promise me, Blanche, you stay there until I come and get you."

"I promise."

Isabelle ran over and jumped into Rye's arms. "Please

come back. I don't want to stay with this woman."

He kissed her on the forehead and whispered to her, "I plan to. I made a promise to your sister, and I don't break my promises."

Blanche touched his face. "Please come back. This time I mean it."

***

Blanche, Isabelle, and Little Deer raced toward Fort Laramie. Blanche thought this may be the end of Rye Tyler, but she wouldn't count on it. The man had a knack for escaping death, but even he couldn't escape what would coming at him. A tear ran down her cheek.

Chapter 29

After the three women took off, Rye climbed on his horse and rode down toward the river and into the mountains toward the southeast. He climbed up the mountain. Once at the top, Rye looked around the area. It looked peaceful for the moment. He stopped at an area to the south and rode down the hill toward what looked like a cave between two cliffs. He couldn't ascend with the horse, so it meant walking up the mountain into the cave.

Rye struggled, but he made it to the cave. He would spend the night here. As Rye warmed himself, he thought of some of Black Elk's last words when he found him.

"I know I will not be in this world much longer. Thank you for doing what you have done, in particular for Little Deer. I have to tell you one last thing before I pass on." The man struggled to get the words out. "That is not her real name."

"What?"

"Little Deer. She is the daughter of a white woman who I kept during a raid many years ago. Her mother is dead, but Little Deer's name is really Emma. Please look after Emma and help her grow to be a wonderful woman."

"I believe she is one right now," Rye told him. "You have done a good job raising your daughter."

That made the Blackfoot chief smile.

Rye asked Black Elk who the young girl's family was. Black Elk shook his head. The only two things he would say was the father had been searching for her. He also told Rye the man would be someone Rye should be wary of.

Black Elk also talked a little bit about Little Deer and how she had changed his life around as a chief. He started to say something more about Little Deer but stopped. Did Little Deer know who the men were who had tried to kill her? That would be something Rye would need to keep in the back of his mind. Rye sat for a few moments thinking about what to do next. It had been at least two hours since Blanche had left. She would have been out of the mountains by now.

Rye twisted his body toward a sound. Sioux language. They had found the horse. He didn't know how many were out there. Rye scrambled out of the cave and quietly slit two throats. He climbed on the horse and chased the Indian ponies away, then headed back into the mountains. Rage sprang up in him once more like it had back during the Civil War. He walked the horse a couple of minutes to give him a breather. Another noise. They weren't Sioux but Confederate soldiers. Rye counted six of them. He lifted his rifle and rapidly shot five times, knocking five off of their horses. The sixth he let live. The man froze, making it easier for Rye to ride down to him. The man had his rifle pointed at him.

He looked with shocked eyes at Rye. "Captain Tyler, you are still alive."

Rye kept his words to himself. Finally, he spoke, "Jeb, go home." Rye turned and rode away. He didn't look back. Once out of sight, Rye thought about what he just did. He could have shot Jeb also. In fact, he had meant to spare him, so he could go back to the Confederate base and tell them to leave. But he dropped that idea when he saw Jeb. Rye had met the man on a farm in Tennessee. He'd saved him and his family, causing Jeb to join the Confederate Army.

Rye rode another hour when he came up to a stream. He stepped off his horse to fill up his canteen with water. A twig snapped, and he swung around with his pistol firing on target, knocking a Confederate soldier down. Screaming across the stream were at least half a dozen Indians—not Sioux, but another tribe Rye had not seen before.

He swung up on his horse and skirted toward the east, away from the warriors. Rye came to a mountain pass and had to climb up quickly to escape from the Indians. After about fifteen minutes, Rye lost them in a maze of mountains. Rye climbed off the horse to give him a rest. He peered down at the warriors, searching for signs of the direction he had gone. Coming up the other side was another group. These looked like Confederate soldiers. He would have to leave the horse here.

Rye started hiking higher into the mountain as the unknown warriors continued up behind him. He reached the point where he had nowhere to go. He would have to make a stand here.

The first set of Indians came up. Rye waited until he could see more of them before firing his rifle. He killed at least three of them. Others had dropped out of sight. The sun went down giving Rye an advantage against the Indians. Many tribes would not fight in the dark.

The Confederates were another story. They would have heard the shots and would make their way up to the same location. Nothing materialized overnight. The morning would be different. It would be an all-out fight. The odds were stacked against Rye, but it had been like that his whole life.

He did get some sleep but woke up early. Rye surveyed the area. It shocked him at what he saw. In the valley at least a dozen men dressed in Confederate uniforms were camped below the mountain where he had camped the night before.

There were no signs of warriors or Confederates on the mountains. He realized why within a moment. A cannon had been fired toward the mountain, falling just short. It would only be a matter of time before the coordinates would be exact, and a round would blast him and this mountain apart.

Rye tried to return down the way he came up. Rifle fire

stopped him from moving any further. He thought about Libbie. Where could she be? He should have taken her in Minnesota and left forever. It had been a mistake. Now that mistake put him in this predicament and most likely would cost him his life.

Another round hit the side of the mountain, shaking it and causing him to lose his balance. The next one hit dead-on, spiraling Rye down the side of the mountain into a crevice.

Chapter 30

Rye screeched in pain knowing the impact had broken his leg. Then everything went black. When he woke up, he looked at his leg, which was bent backwards. Blood flowed out also. He dared not move because he heard voices near him. For some reason whoever had been looking for him had failed to see him. He held his breath as men searched above.

One Confederate said, "it looks like we finally got the bastard."

Another voice spoke up. Marcus Duncan's. "I wanted to be the one to kill him, but if we can't find him, there's no way he could survive. He's probably buried in the rubble somewhere."

For another fifteen minutes, Rye lay quietly. When he felt the men had gone away, he looked at his leg again. Rye had to find a way to straighten it out. It wouldn't be easy. Then it came to him. It would be difficult, but he could use the crevice to snap it the other way. He struggled to the area. It took him a good portion of the morning to get the leg situated. He stuck it into the crevice and jerked it. The pain made him pass out.

***

It took eight days until Blanche, Isabelle, and Little Deer finally rode into Fort Laramie. On the way Black Elk had passed on. Riding into the fort, Blanche noticed the troops preparing for something. She didn't know what it could be.

The women turned at a voice. "Welcome to Fort Laramie," Beth said. "It is great to see you again. Where is Rye?"

"He is in the mountains. I need to see your dad immediately."

The girl must have read Blanche's terrified face and ran with her to her father's office. Once in there, Blanche explained about the situation. The colonel didn't say anything at first but smoothed his mustache. His daughter made up his mind, reminding him how the man had saved her life.

Within minutes at least fifty men prepared to ride to the Bighorn Mountains. The colonel asked her once more where he might be. Blanche explained what she could.

"I can take you there," Little Deer said.

Blanche grabbed her. "You can't go back out there."

"I can help save him. Black Elk is dead. I will do what I can to save him just like he did for my Indian father."

The colonel gave the young girl a horse. She climbed up on it bareback. Little Deer looked down at Blanche. "I will bring Rye back."

"You should be careful yourself."

The captain led the troops out. He bent down next to Blanche. "It is great to see you again. I've missed you."

"Please be careful," she whispered. "Whatever you do. Don't let anything happen to him. We still need him."

***

Isabelle stood with Beth watching the interchange between Blanche and the captain. She couldn't hear what had been said but it had to be no good. She did not trust that woman.

***

The company headed out the gate. Blanche shielded her eyes until they were out of sight. Both of the colonel's daughters were standing next to the woman who had saved them. Isabelle stood to the other side of them. All her life she

210

had been cast aside. This didn't surprise her. Only Rye and Christina had cared for her.

Isabelle glanced up when Beth walked over to her.

"They will get to him in time," Beth said.

"I sure hope so."

The colonel fumed. "This is highly irregular to send a young girl with a troop after a known deserter and spy who should be shot on sight."

Beth touched his arm. "Father, without that man you wouldn't have us here to make you laugh and for sure cook your meals for you."

The man patted his daughter on the head. "You're right."

***

Rye woke up again, the pain excruciating. He stared at his leg. The crevice had helped snap it back into place. Still bones stuck up. Rye tried to put them back in place. It took him some time and many suppressed screams, but it looked like he'd succeeded. Rye wrapped the leg with part of his shirt. He hunted around for something to stabilize the leg. No luck.

He tried to stand up but couldn't. Rye slowly slid along the rocks, and that seemed to work. He stopped and took in his surroundings. Despite the pain, Rye had a few things going for him.

The valley was empty, meaning everyone had disappeared. Second, it would be a struggle, but he could reach the cabin. Finally, it had been a week since Rye had led the Confederates and Indians away from Blanche and the others. They should be at Fort Laramie by now. While Blanche may not send help, Isabelle would make sure someone came to find him. Rye just had to survive until someone found him.

He continued sliding along the crevice working his way back up the mountain. It took him the whole day to return to the location he'd been at before he fell. He would camp here again tonight. Rye had no choice. He fell right asleep.

The next morning the brightness of the sun woke him up. A good night's sleep had helped regain some strength, but he had a long way to go. He studied his leg. It didn't look good. He had to get the inflammation down.

Rye stretched his leg out and propped it up on a rock. He planned to stay where he sat until he the inflammation went down. Rye settled himself into a location where he could see all around him. Yesterday, there was a major movement around the valley. Today, everything was quiet.

Rye had no clue where those men were heading, but they were hiding somewhere out in the mountains. He didn't understand how any of the tribes would fight with Confederates. They would treat them horribly. The tribes were getting themselves involved with something they didn't understand. But then again, Rye thought the tribes were resorting to last-ditch efforts, knowing it would be their last stand.

Rye could relate to their dilemma. He had started his quest—hunting the men who killed the poor souls in Murfreesboro. Then he saw Libbie once more, and that had changed everything. He wanted to escape and start over. He should have trusted his gut and took Libbie away. Why hadn't he? His only thought had been she had forgotten him and found someone else. But he also had thought about someone else.

Then he decided to set his course with Blanche. At first, Rye had hoped he could settle down with her. But things didn't feel right with her from the start. She kept him at a distance in some things but tried to keep him close to her in others. It all revolved around what had been happening to her in the Bighorns.

It boiled down to the fact that Blanche had been given the task with getting Rye out here any way she could. He went along because he thought Libbie had been out of his life for good. After the passionate kiss with her when he tried to escape, he'd been wrong. She still cared about him.

Now, he didn't know where they had taken Libbie. His course had changed once more. No matter what, he would find her. Then he would decide where to go from there.

Rye continued gazing at the valley. He didn't have anything to do throughout the day except to bring down the inflammation in his leg. After a bit, Rye fell asleep.

***

Isabelle sat on the porch of the quarters the colonel had given to her. Without Christina and Rye, she felt alone. Blanche wanted nothing to do with her. She probably wished Isabelle would go away. Isabelle didn't know what to think about Little Deer yet. She had been nice to her, but lots of people had been nice.

"How do you like staying at the fort?"

Isabelle glanced up at the woman called Beth. "I've been to Fort Ridgely before."

"Is that where you met Rye?"

She nodded. "He saved my sister, my brother, and me."

"Mind if I sit down here by you?"

Isabelle nodded. Beth sat by Isabelle. "He saved my sister and my life also. Rye seems to do things like that."

They both smiled at each other.

"I know it is hard for you out here without a family."

"I'm glad you have a family."

Beth smiled. "If the truth be known. my sister, like your sister, Christina, is all I have."

"What about your father?"

Beth looked around before she spoke. "I don't know about him. He hates Rye."

"How could he?"

"I don't know, Isabelle, but he does. I do know one thing. I'm like you and trust Rye Tyler."

***

Rye woke up with a start. The wind had picked up and blew through the mountains. It looked like the swelling had gone down. He tried to stand up. Still no luck. Rye started to crawl around the rocks. After a few moments, he crawled to a dead end.

He gazed around the mountain for a few moments, trying to find an easier way down. Rye's eyes settled on a location that looked like he could make it through. He started crawling once more—this time down the opposite way he had come from. He tried to stand. He managed to do so for a bit but fell back down, sliding down the mountain. He tumbled down out of control, his body bouncing off the rocks until he landed on the floor of the valley. It felt like every bone in his body was busted.

Worse yet, the sound of voices and horses echoed through the valley. He rolled over into the rocks. At least a dozen Sioux warriors rode past, all painted. It dawned on Rye the Indians routinely made their treks through this valley.

Rye lay quietly on the ground until the group had disappeared. He tried to get up on his leg once more. He succeeded but couldn't stay up because he didn't have anything to hold onto. Rye fell right back down onto the ground. He needed a plan. What did he have? His pistol and bullets. His rifle was lost in the crevice. Rye needed to find food and water. He also needed to find a place for protection.

Rye searched around the area until he saw something he could use to help him. Fifty feet ahead of him was a broken tree limb lay on the ground. He crawled toward the limb.

He stopped and looked up. A dozen warriors were staring at him. Several looked up the mountain pass where he had tumbled down. All but one turned and rode away. He stared at Rye. They remembered each other. The Crow rode past him. Rye's eyes followed him.

The Crow stopped, reached down, and picked up the limb. He rode up to Rye and dropped the limb in front of him. The Crow looked up the mountain once more. He started to turn away and stopped. In English, he said. "No one has ever survived falling off the mountain."

The Crow spurred the horse into a gallop. The limb would help, but a horse would have been better. Damn Indians, he smiled to himself. Rye sat down and searched for a sharp rock. A knife would do the job, but he didn't happen to have one on him at the moment.

Rye started to whittle the limb to shape it into something that would help him stand up and give him support for his knee. It took him some time. He had to take breaks because he lost his strength, but he finally finished it. Rye used the limb to stand up. At first, it had been difficult to get used to standing with the limb; even more difficult trying to walk with it. He finally got the hang of it and started on his way. He chose to walk south.

Over the next couple of days, he struggled through the valley. Different Indian tribes continued traveling through. He made sure he stayed out of their sight. Rye fell asleep in a group of rocks. When he woke up the next morning, a dead bird lay near him. He couldn't figure out what happened until he limped over to it. The bird's neck had been broken.

He didn't even think about cooking it. He just ate it raw. It tasted awful, but Rye needed food. Rye also needed something to drink. He started to climb up on his limb when another group of Indians came through the valley.

They stopped and stared at him. Rye couldn't take them all on, but they would not take him alive. One of the warriors came toward him. A Sioux. Rye braced himself. The Indian stopped a few feet away, reached for something, and threw his water pouch toward Rye. He hurried away.

Rye reached for it and drank thirstily. He looked toward the Sioux with a nod. Once he had taken the drink, they headed through the valley. Rye finished the raw bird, swung the water pouch over his shoulder, and continued hobbling. It took forever to cover a few yards.

The fifth day after falling down the mountain, Rye's body gave out. He collapsed in the middle of the valley. The pain in his leg finally took its toll. He lay there staring up at the sky and fell asleep right where he lay. The next morning, he looked up. Indians stared down at him. He had no idea what tribe they came from.

"Just end it," he said to them.

They didn't understand what he told them. Rye let out a deep sigh. No one moved. They turned toward the sound of a bugle. The warriors still didn't move. Finally, they dashed away when soldiers came into view. With another bugle blast, the soldiers charged after them. The Indians disappeared before the troop could catch them.

Someone shook him. "Wake up, Rye."

He must be dreaming. He squinted toward Little Deer, who continued shaking him with tears in her eyes. "Please wake up. You are safe now."

Rye scowled, "Go away. Let me die in peace." Then he fell back to sleep.

Chapter 31

Had he been dreaming or had he died and gone to heaven? He opened his eyes toward the most beautiful woman in the world. It was not the same woman he had seen before, but it looked a lot like her. A soft voice said, "I am so sorry. Things are not what they seem. Please hang in there. We'll be together."

He woke with a start. Blanche slept next to him in a chair. He studied her for a moment. How could it be her in his dream?

She must have felt his eyes staring at her because she smiled at him. "You're alive." Isabelle moved close.

"How long have I been here?"

"You've been sleeping for the last two weeks."

Rye struggled to sit up. Blanche rose to help Isabelle prop him up. It was a struggle, but the two managed. He glanced down at the cast on his leg.

"Your leg will be fine. You broke it in at least three places, but the doctor said for some reason it healed properly."

Rye didn't say anything. He tried to walk but needed help from Blanche and Isabelle.

"You will be able to regain your full motion soon. We'll be here for as many weeks as it takes to heal properly."

Rye hobbled a bit more. "Can you help me outside?"

"Yes," Blanche said.

The three walked out the front door. He took in the

whole fort. Everyone stopped when the three appeared.

"What is happening?"

"I don't know," Blanche said.

Little Deer came running up to him. She gave him a big hug. "I'm glad that you are alive."

He peered at the young girl. "Little Deer, I am so sorry that your father didn't survive, Emma."

All three looked at him.

"What are you talking about, Rye?" Blanche asked.

"It's a long story. Did they take care of Black Elk's body?"

"Crow carried him back to his tribe."

"Can we find a place to sit?"

Blanche and Little Deer helped him back to a bench. He smiled at Little Deer and reached for Isabelle, pulling her up near him.

"Black Elk told me this story before he died. Your real name is Emma. Black Elk took your mother in a raid. Your mother died. Being Black Elk's daughter, the Blackfeet accepted you into the tribe."

A tear rolled down Emma's cheek. "I kind of knew that," she said. "I am not surprised. I am just happy that you are alive."

"What happened to the Confederates and to the Sioux and the others?"

"They have disappeared."

"Why?"

"No one knows."

Over the next ten days, with the help of Isabelle and Emma, Rye started to regain his strength. The colonel's daughters visited regularly. The colonel stopped by once or twice to see him. Rye could tell he really didn't like the idea of his presence at Fort Laramie. He couldn't figure out why.

The post doctor still couldn't believe how well Rye's leg healed. Within a week he could walk without a crutch.

Almost a month after arriving back at the fort, Rye and

Blanche received an invitation to attend a party. Rye couldn't attend because of his leg, but he encouraged Blanche to attend. She did so with reservations at first, then she suddenly became excited about going. A few days later, Blanche came out of the bedroom where they were staying in the officer's quarter. She twirled around in a beautiful red dress.

Rye gazed at her. "You are beautiful, Blanche."

"Am I?" she blushed.

"Yes. Go enjoy yourself."

***

When Blanche walked into the ballroom, everyone gazed at the woman in red. She cast a warm smile at the other guests. She belonged here. The colonel's daughters greeted her, as well as the colonel and his wife.

"How is Rye doing?"

"He seems to be getting better," she said while scanning the whole room. Her eyes stopped on a man who stood in the corner. She knew that face. Rye's brother. The one he didn't know about. More importantly, the man she loved or at least she had loved.

He strolled over to her. "Blanche Davis, how have you been?

She didn't know what to say. "How are you, Preston"

"I'm doing fine now that you're here. You are still as beautiful as ever."

She blushed.

"How long have you been here?"

"I arrived a couple of weeks ago."

They stood next to each other staring at the band. "Would you like to dance?" the man asked.

Blanche smiled. "Of course, I would."

***

Beth slipped out of the party, intending to check on Rye. She hurried to the officer's quarters and knocked on the door. Emma answered it.

219

"May I come in?" she smiled.

Emma nodded. Beth looked over at Rye. "Do you feel better?"

"Much better. Thank you. I had been thinking about trying to go to the dance. Would you allow me to escort you?"

"I would be delighted. You are the handsomest man on the post." Beth winked at Isabelle, who offered a cheerful smile.

Rye glanced at Emma. "I'm going to try to go to the dance."

She grinned at him. "I will help you also."

"I will be proud to be your escort." Rye turned to Beth. "That is, if it's okay with Beth."

"Absolutely."

Emma turned toward Isabelle. "Would you like to come?"

Isabelle shook her head. "I've never been to a dance. I'm way too young"

"I haven't either, Isabelle."

The trio slowly made their way to the dance. Rye opened the door and stepped in behind Beth and Emma. He glanced around the room until he saw Blanche talking to a man he had never seen before. The man's back was turned to him so Rye didn't get a good look at him. For some reason, he felt a twinge of pain in his chest.

"Are you okay, Rye?" Beth asked.

Rye didn't say anything, but his eyes travelled to Blanche. Beth followed his gaze. She touched Rye. "It is better you're not associated with her."

Rye peered at Beth. "What do you mean?"

"That man has been waiting around the fort for the past couple of weeks. My understanding is he's been waiting for someone. Now that I see them together, I think she's the one.

"I'll be right back." Emma walked toward them and stopped. The man was asking Blanche to dance.

He took her hand and they went out onto the dance floor. The man pulled her close to his chest. Her body blended into his. Rye knew what he needed to do. He awkwardly turned around, waved goodbye to Beth, and walked out the door.

***

As the dance ended, Preston kissed her.

She whispered to him. "Please don't do that."

"Not too much longer. It will be over, and my little brother will be dead."

"He doesn't know anything about you. I made sure of that. I'm surprised you're here."

"I'm handling the trading post and dabbling in other things."

"Such as?"

"Things that may lead to us gaining control of the West."

"I can't wait."

He kissed her again. She broke away from him and ran out the door. She should be happy but instead tears brimmed. Once outside the door, Blanche stopped and peered around. This man loved her and would kill Rye; everyone else was too afraid of the man to do it. Now, she wasn't sure if she wanted that to happen.

Chapter 32

Blanche marched into the officer's quarters where she saw Emma consoling Isabelle. "Where is Rye?"

"He's gone."

"What?" Blanche cried.

"He saw you with that man and turned around and left."

"Where did he go?"

"I don't know. There was sadness in his eyes. I asked him to stay, but his eyes looked dead. He hugged Isabelle, told her he would be back, and he left."

Emma hesitated. "I thought you loved Rye. Not another man."

Blanche sat down, tears streaming down her cheeks. She had really screwed everything up.

***

After Rye had seen the interaction with Blanche and the man at the dance, he hurried as best he could to the stable. He saddled the Black and rode through the open gate. The guards didn't stop him or say a word.

Rye headed toward the mountains. He needed to think. More importantly he needed to get away from everything. Things were coming to a head. The man Blanche had been dancing with played a big part of everything that would happen soon. Rye would play along to figure out what it all meant.

Worst of all he felt lonely once more, which was nothing new. The loneliness would remain until he found Libbie.

He headed toward the mountains with no destination in mind. It had been the one place he truly enjoyed; one of the few things he had been truthful to Blanche about. He dearly loved these mountains. Perhaps it was the only place he'd find peace.

Rye had been fooling himself. Only Libbie could help straighten out his life. The problem was—he had no idea how to find her. His gut told him the mountains would be the place to search. He stopped for a moment. Before he died, he would find her. Rye hadn't done much right in his life. Finding her would be the one thing he did right.

***

Blanche woke up the next morning. She didn't know what to do. Rye had slipped right out of her hands. She stepped out of the door to start the search and ran smack into Ben.

"Good morning, Blanche."

"Morning, Ben." She smiled.

"I have to go, but will talk to you later."

"I can't wait," she said touching his hand. Blanche looked after the man. She was playing with fire, but she had to keep the two brothers in line. Now Preston ran the post store. Blanche turned away and went into the colonel's quarters. She explained to him that Rye had left the fort.

"We can't send anyone after him. He's on his own. You can ride with Captain Ben Raven and his detail into Montana if you wish, but that won't be until spring."

"Isn't there anything you can do? Can't you go and find him?"

"Blanche, I have no authority over Rye Tyler. By all rights I should hang him on the spot."

"Even after what he did to help your daughters?"

"My daughters are the only ones keeping him alive."

She started to walk away.

"Blanche, I would not recommend leaving this place. Everyone has orders to keep you from leaving."

"So you're saying the only way I can leave is in the spring."

"That is correct."

Blanche left the office and headed directly back to the quarters. She shook Emma, who was sleeping. "Come on, we need to move."

"What is happening?"

"I screwed up. I have to find Rye and straighten it out."

"Any idea where he may have gone?"

"Back into the mountains and to the cabin."

"That is going to be a dangerous trek for three women."

Blanche smiled at her. "We made it down here. We can make it back up there."

A couple of hours later when Blanche opened the door, a soldier stood out front of the quarters. "Sorry, ma'am, you can't leave the fort."

"What?"

"Colonel's orders. He said to watch over you since you're the captain's wife. It's only until the quarters are arranged."

Blanche frowned at the private, then marched toward the colonel's quarters with the private following her. She walked right into the colonel's office in the middle of a meeting.

He raised his voice. "What the hell are you doing—" The colonel met Blanche at the door. "Please excuse me for a moment, gentlemen."

"Why am I being guarded like I'm a prisoner?"

"That is not happening to you, Blanche Raven."

"What?" she exclaimed.

"Yes, Ben came in and showed me your wedding certificate."

"I am not married to that man."

"That's not what I understand. Weren't you engaged to Ben Raven?"

"No, not to a Ben Raven at any time. That man is not Ben Raven. He is Ben Tyler. You plan on hanging his little brother, Rye, but this man is wicked."

He pulled out a wedding certificate. "That is not what this says. It says you two were married a year ago in Minnesota."

She looked at it. "It's a forgery. I have never been in love with Ben at any time, and I only met him a few times several years ago before being sent away to the East."

"Sorry, Blanche. This says differently."

Blanche spun around and stormed to the door. She stopped to look at the man. "Colonel, the man I have loved since I was ten years old left this fort last night. I will find a way to get back to him. I screwed up by ever getting mixed up with his older brother, Ben Tyler, and broke his heart. I will fix his broken heart."

She stormed out the door.

Chapter 33

Rye pushed up the pace and in five days reached the cabin. He made up his mind—no matter what, let them come. Nothing to lose. He would find Libbie Davis, the only woman he ever loved. Then he'd go back and get Isabelle. Isabelle would be safe at Fort Laramie for the moment. Beth said she would watch over her until he returned.

Once he arrived at the cabin, Rye dropped on a bed and slept for the rest of the day. That night he crawled out of bed and found himself something to eat. He decided to make a plan. The next day he would head further into the mountains and find the remainder of the Confederates and Marcus Duncan. There would be no mercy for Marcus Duncan.

He stepped outside with a cup of coffee and watched the snow slowly come down. A beautiful snow. He stared toward the north. His mind wandered to the woman he loved. The only one he would ever love. Maybe it didn't matter now, because she seemed to be tied up with Marcus Duncan. He wasn't even sure if Blanche cared about him. It seemed a captain stood in the way. He would find out one way or another starting tomorrow.

Rye had a hard time believing Libbie loved Marcus. Or maybe he just did not want to believe it. It really didn't matter now, because the trail he headed down could end his life once and for all.

And he couldn't even imagine why he would be thinking about Blanche. Rye figured she'd been given the job to destroy him. What did they want from him anyway? It had to be gold. He knew how to find it, but he'd die before they'd get any of it.

The next morning Rye headed north and went even further into the mountains. After lunch the third day, he finally came down. He stopped when he saw an area of empty land as far as he could see. Beautiful. It must be a part of the Montana Territory, something he had not seen before.

He took a drink from his canteen and glanced up as a Sioux warrior came flying at him knocking him off his horse. The warrior seemed to be quicker than most Rye had faced. Sioux, as most Indians, were adept at hand-to-hand battle. Rye struggled with him but finally lifted him off the ground, breaking his neck.

That night Rye camped on the open prairie with a fire burning, an invitation for anyone to join him. He didn't care anymore. Three men rode into camp asking for some coffee. Rye provided each a cup. They got up and left. It wasn't but five minutes when the three returned, guns blazing. Rye stood and nailed the first two. He winged the third man. "I'm going to ask you only once. Why did you come back shooting?"

"Simple. Marcus Duncan has put a bounty on your head."

"I see. What about a woman named Libbie Davis?

"Tall beauty. I've seen her. She suddenly disappeared."

"Do you know where?"

The man shook his head. Rye let him go with a message for Duncan: "I'm coming for you." He rolled over into his blanket and fell right asleep.

***

It had been a month since Rye left Fort Laramie. And during those four weeks, Blanche did everything she could to stay away from Preston in public. Much of the time he had been working at the post saloon, but at night the two were able to be together after Emma and Isabelle had gone to bed.

He made it a point to stay as close to Blanche as he could. Blanche knew he could kill Emma and Isabelle and take her anytime he wanted. She couldn't quite comprehend why he didn't. The only thing she could think of was he had a more devious scheme in his mind. But it would never include anything that would harm her.

One night while talking, Blanche brought up Captain Raven and marriage. The man she sat with looked at her. "That is our brother as you well know. I told him to file a certificate of marriage to throw everyone off the trail."

"I see."

May showed signs of spring at the fort. Blanche had been hatching a plan to escape as soon as she could. She would head back to the cabin because she believed Rye would be there. She needed to reach him and keep him close until Ben and the others came for him. At least she thought that until a group of Crow scouts came riding into the post one morning. Nonstop chattering in their native tongue. The one man who could translate had not been on the post. But, Emma had heard everything they said.

"What are they talking about?"

"Rye."

"What?" She frowned at her. "Is he okay?"

"He's okay. But no one survived."

"What are you talking about?"

"Remember my vision. He has spared no one."

"Yes."

"That is what is happening. They say a white man is going berserk in the mountainous country and in Montana. He's hunting for someone. Even the Shoshone are afraid of him. They do not scare easily. It is their country."

"How do you know it is Rye?"

"They all say he has dead eyes. Eight men charged him in a horse fight on the plains and all were dead when the fight ended."

In that zone nothing phased him. She saw that when he

killed four Sioux who charged the two of them. "We have to do something, Emma."

"What? We cannot leave here."

"We have to find a way. If we don't get to him, they will kill him. And it is all my fault."

"I will help you." Emma looked over at Isabelle. "We will help you," she said, smiling at the little girl, the first time Emma had smiled at Isabelle. Isabelle smiled back.

"Rye would want me to stay here."

"Then you stay here," Blanche said. "I'm sure the colonel's daughters will look after you."

Beth and Katie had walked over to where the ladies stood. "I heard what is happening. It can only be Rye," Katie said.

"How do you know it is him?" Blanche asked.

"As soon as you said dead eyes, I knew," Beth said. "I saw them when the Hatcher men tried to rape me. I looked at Rye and saw they were empty. He didn't care."

Beth glanced at Isabelle and took her hand. "Isabelle, Rye wanted me to look after you. We will keep you safe."

"I know you will," Isabelle said.

Chapter 34

Rye came across a mountain top far to the west, further than he had ever been. He stopped the horse when something like the sound of gushing water shot out of the ground. He had never seen anything like what he just witnessed. It wasn't water but steam shooting out of the ground. He stared in awe at how high the steam shot up.

He continued his trek through the mountains heading south. Not a single Indian or white man passed throughout the ride. He headed back toward the cabin to get some rest and regroup.

***

There was no sign of Rye at the cabin when Blanche and Emma arrived a week later.

"Is Rye here?"

"Yes, he has been here."

"How do you know?"

"I feel it."

She looked at the blue dress wrapped on the table.

The front door opened and in walked Rye. He stared at Blanche without a word.

Blanche spoke first, "Rye, I am so sorry. I never meant to hurt you in any way."

Rye still didn't say anything.

"Damn it, You are the man I love. I have loved you as long as I can remember."

Rye noticed Emma's face out of the corner of his eye.

He swung around, palmed his pistol, and plugged a bullet into the head of the man coming through the door. Emma scrambled out of the way. He dove for Blanche and knocked her to the floor. Another man came through the door, and Rye shot him also. "Stay down." Rye raced out the door as another horse started to ride away. A shot came from behind him and a man fell down to his right. He glanced at Emma who had fired the shot that killed him. She dropped the rifle and ran into his arms.

She cried, her whole body shaking. Rye held her tight. "It's okay. You saved my life."

Emma looked up at him and let him lead her to sit on the porch.

Blanche joined him. "Please forgive me, Rye. I can't live my life without you."

"Hell, Blanche, you broke my heart. How can I ever forgive you?" He pushed her away.

Tears streamed down Blanche's face and her bottom lip quivered.

"Where is Isabelle?"

"Beth, the colonel's daughter, is watching her," Emma said.

He started to walk out the door, then stopped "Stay here. I don't care anymore. I'm through with your games." Rye looked at the table. "I bought that blue dress for you. It's your favorite color, but I was wrong about you like everything else in my life. Neither you nor either of our families will turn me."

He climbed on his horse and rode away once more.

Blanche collapsed on the porch, her eyes following the direction Rye had ridden. "I don't know if he'll ever forgive me. I've had horrible dreams that I would have to bury him. The way he's heading, that could happen." She turned toward Emma. "I know you believe dreams are powerful."

Emma's eyes grew large. The young girl took her hand. Blanche smiled. "Blanche, Rye is going to be just fine. You have him totally confused."

Frown lines furrowed Blanche's brow.

"I know a lot about everything. Don't worry, your secret is safe. You will be leaving soon, but I will still be around."

Early the next morning, a cavalry detachment rode into the yard. Captain Ben Raven led the detail. Blanche stood in the doorway glaring at him and the others.

"Captain," she acknowledged.

"Blanche. I'm so glad you are okay. I came to take you home."

Her hand posted on her waist. "I am not going back with you. This is my home. My home is with Rye Tyler, your younger brother."

He looked at her dumbfounded. "My brother?"

"Yes, the one your father and mother sent away to Tennessee when he turned ten."

"He's dead."

"He's not dead."

"Damned Duncan."

"What?" she exclaimed. "You know Duncan?"

"Who do you think orchestrated all this? If I do have a younger brother, it doesn't matter because my job is to bring Rye Tyler or whatever his name is to justice."

"With a dozen men?" Emma laughed. "You won't survive a day out there against him."

The sergeant came up to address the captain, the same sergeant from Minnesota. "It is you again?" Blanche said.

"Howdy, ma'am."

"Don't howdy me, sergeant. You're chasing down the man who saved your life back in Minnesota."

"The man is a murderer."

"A murderer! He is doing the Army's job. The murderers are Marcus Duncan, my father, and you, Ben Raven."

"Let's move, sergeant. I will be back for you."

Emma stood tall. "If you go out there, you'll only return

232

if Rye allows it."

He snickered and led the troop away.

***

The troop had traveled two miles when they came across their first signs. The Crow scout motioned for the captain to step down.

In English, the Crow said it looked like one man went through the trees and had doubled back toward the mountains.

The captain scratched his two-day old stubble of a beard. He asked the scout what he thought.

The Crow hesitated before speaking, "We will only find him if he wants us to find him."

"Bull shit. He is a man."

The Crow shrugged. "If the man called Rye Tyler went up and down this mountain, he is a formidable foe."

"Let's move out toward the mountain where the trail leads."

***

The twelve-man patrol headed to the north and then turned west over the same mountain pass that Christina had dragged Rye over. It turned out to be slow going for the troop.

What they didn't know, the man whom they were searching for was looking down at them. Rye focused his eyeglass at the troop. The captain led the way. It looked like the one who brought Isabelle's parents up to the cabin. He could not kill the man Blanche loved. He had to keep this man alive for Blanche.

He put his eyepiece away, turned the horse around, and headed down away from the troop going over the mountain. At one point, Rye passed within ten feet of the Crow scout. He stopped immediately, sniffing the air.

"Take them back now, or they will all die," Rye whispered to the scout.

***

The voice frightened the Crow. The white man named Rye Tyler passed by. The rest of the troop rode up to the Crow scout. The Indian climbed off his horse and started chanting. It grew louder and louder. Neither the captain nor sergeant could stop it. When he did stop fifteen minutes later, the Crow spoke in English. "We must go or we will die."

"From one man?"

"That one man is dead in his heart. He has nothing to live for. He will kill until he is killed."

***

The men looked around. They'd heard of Shoshone parties coming through and butchering anyone in their sight, especially white men. But they'd never heard of such a white man. The captain glared at the sergeant. The captain did not fear the man but could see the fear in the sergeant's and the others' eyes.

"I have seen him in action, Captain. He is deadly."

"Let's call it a day and head back to the cabin to stay for the night. We'll head back to Fort Laramie and pick up more men."

***

Blanche whirled around, sensing someone behind her. When she turned, Rye stood there. Neither said anything.

"Are you okay?" she asked. She noticed his dead eyes like everyone had said.

"I did not kill him."

"What are you talking about?"

"I did not kill the captain because you are in love with him."

He pivoted and started to walk out the door but stopped, looked at Emma, and turned back to Blanche. "I would never kill the man you love because I do care about you."

Blanche's voice stopped him. "Look at me, damn you. I have followed you hundreds of miles across the country. I have patched you up when you needed it. My heart broke when your heart broke. I came back to this cabin because I am going to spend the rest of my life with you and bear your children."

Rye's expression didn't change. "Blanche, we both know that's never going to happen. The captain is not the man you are in love with. The man you are spending the rest of your life with is still out there. You two danced together. You have shielded him from me. But I will find him."

Rye was almost at the threshold when two shots knocked him down. Emma and Blanche screamed and ran toward him. They both looked on in amazement as Rye pushed up off the floor. He climbed onto his horse and headed west into the mountains.

He had just made it out of sight when the cavalry came racing into the yard.

"Emma, please help me. They can't know. They will chase him down and kill him," Blanche said.

Emma looked at her with a questioning glance. Blanche motioned her to move.

The first one to ride in the yard was the Crow scout. He glanced toward the direction that Rye had gone. He rode over to the porch and spoke to Emma in his native tongue. Her eyes grew large.

"What?" Blanche asked.

"He said he would cover the tracks, so Rye could escape."

"Why would he do that?"

The Crow spoke in broken English. "He could have killed me but chose to allow me to live. I will protect him as long as I breathe. Only a man who cares about life will do that." The Crow headed in the opposite way that Rye had gone. As soon as he started heading east, the patrol came into the yard. Out of nowhere the Shoshone hit the cabin in full force.

Blanche had never seen a Shoshone Indian. In fact, only White Hawk and Emma had seen them. But she had heard stories. She and Emma grabbed rifles and started shooting, helping the detachment make it into the cabin.

A dozen warriors circled the area, all hard to hit because of their movements around the yard. Raven and the sergeant swore because they couldn't hit one warrior after a dozen shots.

"What the hell are they—ghosts?" the captain asked.

Both females gasped when they heard the shots from the outside. "What is happening?"

A giant of a man stood in the doorway. He had a patch on his left eye, his right hand replaced with a hook. "Where's Blanche Davis?"

"Kingman," Blanche exclaimed, looking at the man who filled the doorway. She ran to him. "You are still alive!" Kingman didn't take his eyes off Raven. The two appeared to know each other.

Raven turned to the sergeant and told him to round up the men. "We're heading to Fort Laramie."

As they saddled up, Raven turned to Blanche. "This is not over. You will be my woman one way or another."

Chapter 35

Almost as soon as the detachment left, the Crow scout appeared. When Kingman saw him, both were poised to strike like rattlers. Blanche touched his arm. "No, he saved our lives."

The man called Kingman relaxed. The Crow and he studied each other with narrowed eyes.

"Did you find Rye?"

"No, he wants no one to find him."

She looked at Kingman and smiled. "It is good to have you here. I'm glad you're alive. I don't know how you survived."

He eyed her. "My job is to protect you."

She smiled at him. "Please stay with us?" She turned to the Crow. "Please stay also."

The Crow scout spoke, "My name is White Hawk. Shoshone will return with more warriors. Solid home. We have more to fight with."

***

Rye crawled off his horse once he reached a mountain stream in the mountains. The two bullets had passed through, and that was the only reason he still lived. His life had become one of being riddled with bullets and running from people. He took a few moments to dress his wounds. It hurt a bit, but he would be okay. His horse's ears perked up at a sound just across the river. Rye pulled the Black back out of the way just as half a dozen or more Shoshone moved through.

Just above him were another twelve or so. It looked like a good-sized war party. The only place they could be heading from that direction was the cabin. Rye started to climb off his horse when a Shoshone scout sat on his horse staring at him not ten feet away.

He let out a cry and Rye knew that more would be coming. He climbed on his horse, thumbed his pistol, and killed him instantly. The one thing he could never do was lead the Shoshone back to the cabin.

He headed further west into the mountains.

***

The Crow scout stood watching as the other Shoshone picked up the trail. The man had saved their lives for the time being. Rye Tyler would have no chance against these warriors. The Shoshone could track.

White Hawk turned his horse back toward the cabin once the warriors had passed. He returned to the cabin after dark. He knew the big man hid in the shadows watching him.

Both went inside. The Crow looked at Blanche. "Rye Tyler led them away from here. There are at least two dozen and more coming. He will not survive this time. Too many Indians. They are skilled at this."

Blanche peered at him. "White Hawk, I have seen that man survive things that no human alive can. He will return."

***

Rye had led the Shoshone around their own backyard for at least three days. He came across physical features he never could have imagined—tall mountain peaks, deep water pools, and rapid waterfalls. Once he came across a Shoshone tribe encampment in the middle of the night. The next day he sat quietly watching the scenes of children playing and women singing. Such a peaceful feeling. Rye knew they were watching him. He really didn't care. He continued watching the children play. The sun started to set when a noise came from behind. He spun around with his pistol pointed at the men. They weren't men. Cheyenne Dog Soldiers dressed in even scarier faces than he had seen earlier.

"Rye Tyler, you are away from your family."

"I have no family," he said to the one who had spoken.

"Then you are like the Cheyenne Dog Soldiers. We will have no family either. The war will end in the other part of the country, and the White Eyes will bring it to us. Our world will be wiped out."

"Why are you in Shoshone territory?" Rye asked.

"Rye Tyler, we are Cheyenne Dog Soldiers. We fear no one." The speaker turned and started to ride away. Then he stopped and turned toward him. "The only man we fear is you." The Cheyenne Dog Soldiers rode away into the dark.

On the fifth day, Rye knew he had lost the Shoshone who had been following him. The Dog Soldiers had scared them off. He would head back, find out what he could, and then get Isabelle. Then the two of them would search for Libbie. Late on the third night he arrived back at the cabin.

Rye crept inside and stood looking around. A big man slept on the couch and the Crow was nowhere in sight. Rye had known the Crow followed him.

Rye walked toward the bedroom where Emma would be sleeping quietly and opened the door. No Emma. She must be sleeping elsewhere. He whirled around ready to sleep out in the barn. Then he noticed the blue dress sitting where it had been.

"Where are you going, Rye?"

"What are you still doing up, Emma?"

She smiled at him. "You're not here, so someone has to stand watch over this group."

"They couldn't have picked a better person." He smiled back.

Rye turned to walk out the door. "You promised you would protect Isabelle."

"I know. Isabelle is not here."

"Then why leave?"

"It's not that easy. I'm a murderer and will die that way sooner or later. I don't want anything to happen to her."

"Don't you think we know who you are? You've saved all of our lives at one time or another. Now it is time to let us protect you."

"You have a kind heart, but it doesn't work that way. I have to find Libbie. I need her to keep me from destroying myself."

He headed toward the barn to grab his horse but stopped. On the porch stood Emma, now a young sixteen-year-old girl with tears streaming down her cheeks, gazing at him hoping that he would stay. He thought for a moment and then led the horse into the barn.

"Let us help you," Emma said. "You say you need Libbie. I need you, Rye. I have no one and neither does Isabelle. And if truth be known, neither does Blanche."

"You win," he said ruffling her hair.

"I knew you'd do the right thing."

Rye kissed Emma on the cheek and walked out to the barn. He lay down on the straw and fell asleep immediately.

***

The next morning, Blanche woke up early like she always did. She walked out on the porch to look in all directions. It made her feel comfortable knowing that the man she loved was out there and would come home someday.

She turned around as Kingman came walking out. He towered over her by at least a foot. With Kingman here, things would start to come together. The destruction of Rye Tyler had begun. She had decided she couldn't be part of it, but how could she convince Rye? Blanche wandered out to the barn to check on the horses. She stopped as the rifle pointed at her.

"You sure like the comfort of straw, don't you?"

He sat up. "I always come to places like this to clear my

head. It helps me think."

"And what have you been thinking about?"

"How beautiful you look in a blue dress."

She smiled at him. "Blue is my favorite color. For some reason you knew that, but that is not what you are thinking about."

"When they sent me away, I felt alone and worthless. During the war, I felt no one could love me because I had turned into a murderer and really didn't give a damn. I kept hoping someone would end my misery. At times I enjoyed it...until now. When I butchered each one of those men over the past month or so, I wasn't doing it for any other reason than to relieve my frustrations. I never wanted to be alone again, so I thought it was easier to hope that someone would kill me.

"The only reason I keep coming back is to make sure Emma is okay. Every time I did that, I kept hoping I wouldn't die. If I keep going the way I am, it will happen. And what is happening is tied to you, Libbie, and Marcus Duncan. I do see Libbie in many of my dreams. She is not there for me. You are. There is also someone out there whom I can't see at this point."

He paused for a moment. "You are fortunate I didn't stick around to see who you had been dancing with. If I had, I would have looked into the eyes of my older brother, the one who will be tormenting me until I end it. There will be another time."

Blanche sat next to him in the straw. "I don't know where we will go next. My family is evil. Your family is the devil. You are of that breed, but the difference is you have a kind heart, and you have shown that many times. The latest is the Crow scout, White Hawk. You let him live. And you shouldn't have." Blanche hesitated, tears trickling from her eyes. "Marcus Duncan told me if I didn't do everything he told me to do, they'd hunt you down and do worse than they ever did to Kingman. Then he sent the three men after you to have you killed anyway." She peered at him. "I'm so sorry you had to go through all of this. It will never be over if that man is alive. But if it's going to end, you will be the one to determine how it does."

"Why are you holding things back from me? You keep telling me I'm part of this plan. What is this plan? If it's the gold bullion you're searching for, I'll die first. The only thing I want to know is—where is Libbie?"

"I don't know, and that's the truth."

"Even if you did know, you wouldn't tell me."

"You're right, I wouldn't. And why should I? You don't seem to get it. It's more than Libbie."

"No, Blanche, you don't understand. It is all Libbie. It's always been about Libbie. She's kept me going wherever I've been. I should have taken her to Minnesota, then none of this would be happening. She and I could have just disappeared off the face of this earth."

"Why didn't you?"

Rye didn't respond.

"Do you really know who she is, Rye? She's a rich woman. You are a poor man who's turned into a killer. She'll never stoop to the likes of you. You have a better chance with the woman called Beth at the fort. I can tell she's in love with you, or is it she feels safe around a murderer? Or the young woman, Christina. She's more like you than you realize. You both are nobodies."

Rye glared at her. "I am just plain tired. And you're a bald-faced liar. You and I will never part until either I'm dead or I find Libbie. And for your sake and the sakes of those you hang around, nothing had better happen to her."

"Or what? You'll kill everyone? You haven't figured it out. There have been many times where I or others could have ended your life just like that." She snapped her fingers. "Do you think Little Deer or Isabelle just showed up? We didn't kill you because we need your help. Libbie will be the one who kills you. And that will be poetic justice. She's changed in the past dozen years. We've all changed in the past dozen years. And not for the better."

Blanche hesitated for a moment. Then a tear ran down her eye. She wiped it away and glanced at Rye. "You're right. I have lied to you. I've manipulated you in any way possible. You're also right about the captain who came into the cabin. I knew him from before. He's one of your older brothers, Ben. The man you saw me dancing with at the post is your oldest brother, Preston."

She hesitated once more. "Preston and I are to be married soon. But I don't know if I want to marry him."

"Why?"

Blanche squeezed Rye's hand tighter. "I'm the youngest Davis daughter, not Libbie. You never knew about me because my last name is Park like I said when you first saw me. I'm the daughter of a woman Davis slept with. I have no idea where they sent her. They've shielded me from you in the hope that you'll tell me where the gold bullion is that everyone is searching for. They all believe you've stolen it and know where it is. My job is to find out where it is in any way I can.

"I never thought you would be such a complicated man. One minute you can kill with ease, the next minute you're as kind as can be. You are like no man I've ever met. You are not a Tyler or a Davis. The problem is they will never stop coming after you because of that gold. Libbie will continue to lead the charge. She is the mastermind of all this, along with your oldest brother, Preston, and the old man you should have killed in the cabin."

"That's not true, Blanche."

"I'm telling you the truth, Riley Tyler. You are completely wrong about Libbie. She's been married for two years to a man called Wil Cason. You know him because he's the one you assigned to protect her over the years. He'll come for you as others will; men and women you would never expect will try to kill you. This is more than about gold bullion. Everyone believes you have secrets that will destroy each one of them. For all I know, as crazy as our families are, they could believe you have the secrets to immortality. That is why Duncan sent three men to kill you in Tennessee. They were more willing to risk not finding the gold than to have you tell all their dirty little secrets."

Rye stared at the young woman. "I have no idea about any secrets. Why are you telling me this now? Why should I believe any of this at all?"

"I know I've never given you any reason to believe I'm telling you the truth. But I am. I never expected this at all. I figured you were a crazy man like the rest of our family, and you'd be glad to provide the gold to everyone, so they could become even richer than they are. Rye Tyler, I never expected to fall in love with you."

Rye hesitated for a moment, then spoke, "I could have left and never been found anytime I wanted in the past year. I had my own reasons why I continued to come back. Sure, I wanted to check on Isabelle, but I also wanted to make sure you were okay. Every time I returned, I kept telling myself this is nuts, I can't fall in love with a woman who wants to destroy me. But I did. And now you tell me that you love me." He stared at her for the longest time, studying her eyes. "I believe you are telling me the truth." A smile swept across his face and he shook his head. "You know that we will never have any peace, and every day will be an adventure?"

***

Blanche didn't say anything. Rye pulled her to his chest and kissed her passionately on the lips. She responded with the same amount of fervor. Finally, she broke away, breathless. The kiss had touched her heart. "Whoa, what a way to start an adventure." She walked away touching her cheek. She needed some fresh air.

THE END

Author Bio: My wife, Susan and I have two sons, Justin (Kayla) and Jeremy and a grandson, Aiden. Born and raised in South Dakota. I enjoy spending time with family, traveling and putt-putt. I am currently the managing editor of a small town Iowa newspaper. I am a former Marine Corps veteran, getting my start in the publishing business in 1981 working for several years on base newspapers. I spent time running my own freelance business. I love writing. I enjoy reading anything and everything. I also love the history of our country and enjoy reading western books, mysteries, and adventure novels, and watching mystery, adventure, and western movies.

Made in the USA
Columbia, SC
19 February 2021

33156307R00150